SING THE
COWS HOME

"The summer I was eleven years old,
I was alone at our fäbod, taking care of
four cows, two heifers and the goats.
One of my heifers had a calf, so I was
alone when she had to be milked for
the first time. I was so scared I cried.
Finally I got up enough courage and
sat down beside her and stroked her
udder very gently, and as I did that she
stuck out her tongue and began licking
me, intensely, on my arm. If they lick
you, then you know they are nice."
— Liss Anna

Kerstin Brorson

Sing the Cows Home

Welcome Press   1985   Seattle

Sing the Cows Home
Copyright © 1985
Welcome Press

ISBN 0-916871-07-X

Illustrations: Hearth cabin interior
page 21 Nordiska Muesst, Stockholm; photos pages 53, 63, 68, 69,
Dalarnas Museum, Falun, Sweden;
other photos by author. Pen and
ink, Kris Ekstrand Molesworth.

Welcome Press
2701 Queen Anne Avenue North
Seattle, Washington 98109

CONTENTS

PREFACE

The summer pastures of both Swedish and Norwegian farm life of the past have long been a romantic theme of Nordic literature. Mention the seters of Norway or the fäbod of Sweden and one conjures up pictures of flaxen-haired women in long skirts and white aprons blowing their lur against a background of white-capped mountains.

But what has escaped us is the rich well of folklore that evolved from this summer work, especially as it related to the herdswomen themselves. Nor have we comprehended the tremendous responsibility laid on the women and young girls who cared for the cattle all summer, or the unique position it gave them in their village or community.

In this book the herdswoman comes into her own. Author Kerstin Brorson explores not only the setting of isolation, heavy work and singular responsibility at the summer pastures, but also the effect it had on the women and girls themselves.

Cowherds in most other cultures have been men. Brorson suggests that this may have been true at one time in Sweden as well. A royal ordinance in 1686 strongly suggests that farmers who have women capable of taking care of the cattle should not let men or boys do the herding. Swedish writer Montelius belives this was "part of a systematic endeavor to engage women in economic responsibility for the farm, which would free men for active service in the army."

Keeping the cows up in mountain pastures through the summer was an economic necessity in certain areas of both Sweden and Norway in early times. Before the breakthrough of modern technology, there was seldom enough food to feed the population adequately. Fields around the village were small and every inch was needed to grow grain crops during the short summer. But the protein-rich milk products were extremely important, and meadows had to produce enough hay to keep the cows alive through the long winter. Other means had to be found to pasture the cows through the summer, and so the woods, bogs, and occasional grasslands of the mountains came to be used, both for grazing and for hay.

Because women cared for the cows and did the milking at home, it was logical that they should go with them to the mountains in summer, leaving the men free to plant and harvest the grain crops and put up the winter's supply of hay. Men would sometimes help the women if there was any great danger from wolves or bears, or in the fall when the cows would wander off searching for mushrooms. But if a man herded all summer it was considered a curiosity.

The resilience and independence developed by these women, some of whom began herding alone as early as 11 years, is amazing. But even more amazing is the psychological tie that made the mountain experience almost a spiritual thing. Even today, after almost all the summer herding cabins have been converted to summer retreats, older women will go up to look around, start a fire in the old fireplace, drink a cup of coffee and savor the old memories that return. They may handle an old spoon or utensil, they may even sing a snatch of their old herding calls, those wordless ancient tunes which open-endedly vibrated among the trees long ago. They feel deeply this active folklore tie to days past. Younger members of the family sense in the old **fåbod** a connection of one generation with another, a sense of belonging, a feeling of being part of a continuous culture.

Although Kerstin Brorson wrote "Sing the Cows Home" as a field study of the folklore surrounding the **fåbod** in the Dalarna section of Sweden, the book goes far beyond this. Because the environment shaped not only these remarkable women but also the folklore that developed around them, Brorson brings us into the very setting itself — the cabins, the sheds, the utensils, the cows, the cheese-making, the exciting trek to the mountains in spring and the happy cheese-and-butter-laden return in the fall.

Two words will become so familiar to you that, in the remainder of this book, we have chosen not to italicize them. The summer buildings for a herder and cattle came to be called **fåbod** (pronounced feh-bood), from **få** (animals) and **bod** (building). The plural form is **fåbodar**. Actually, the correct, standard Swedish word would be **fåbodställe** (cattle building complex), but the shortened version has become acceptable. Several other dialect versions of the word are used in different parts of Dalarna.

The women who lived at the fåbod and cared for the animals will be called **vallkulla** (**väl** means to herd).

Kerstin Brorson, born in Sweden, finished Teachers College in Linköping before moving to the U.S. She holds a bachelor's degree in Anthropology from the University of California Berkeley and has taught elementary school in California and Colorado. She recently received her master's degree in Folklore from San Diego State University. She is presently director of the Swedish American Museum in Philadelphia. This book's first printing was under the name Kerstin Brashers; with this second printing she resumes the use of her Swedish family name.

CHAPTER ONE

BACKGROUND:

GEOGRAPHICAL, HISTORICAL, ECONOMIC

In order to understand the folklore of the Swedish fäbod, we must understand some of the conditions that produced it. The geographical, historical, and economic influences on fäbod life placed demands on the inhabitants and called out qualities of personality and character that are peculiar to the area. This personality and character were, in turn, modified by the traditions and customs of the area and by the economic necessities that geography and climate imposed. Dalarna's fäbod life was no exception. The vallkullor's personality was shaped by the physical environment, by history and customs, and by the necessity of making a living in a hard land.

WHAT IS DALARNA LIKE?

In the Scandinavian peninsula, Norway has almost all of the high mountains, leaving Sweden with rolling, forest-covered mountains which seldom reach over 3000 feet. The Ice Age left its mark; it scraped off the mountain tops and filled the valleys with a morain layer of fractured rocks of varying sizes. Glacial rivers deposited ridges of boulders running roughly in a north-south direction. The glaciers also dug holes and left deposits which created thousands of small lakes which dot the landscape. Because of these geographic features, large scale farming is found only south of the fäbod area.

A large part of Sweden and about 74 percent of Dalarna are covered by forests. Montelius points out that

> "the forest was the area where practically all the feed for the animals was gathered—summer feed on the grazing areas, winter feed through hay-making in meadows and on bogs and through gathering leaves. The forest's significance for Dalarna's farm communities' food supply in the past can hardly be overestimated. The forest was the stable foundation upon which the entire economic life depended."

Another 7 percent of the province is taken up by farmland, and the rest by bogs, lakes, and sloping mountaintops above the timberline. The forest is mostly coniferous, dominated by pine and spruce. The birches are by far the most common of the deciduous trees. The dwarf birch grows about two feet tall on the edge of the bogs and above timberline between 2400 and 3000 feet. A few other deciduous trees dot the forests: alder and aspen and mountain ash.

The quality of the forest is determined in part by the soil condition and the climate. The most northern part of the province has slow-growing trees that do not get as tall as in the southern parts.

Large sections of slow-growing forest north of Lake Siljan grow on rather dry and sandy moors, covered by a dry white moss (**cladonia rangiterina**). This area does not provide as good grazing as the area around and south of Lake Siljan, where the soil has more lime deposits and more ground water available, giving a greener and thicker forest. The ground is covered not only by grass, but also by blueberries, lingonberries and an abundance of wild flowers, ferns, and herbs.

The forests are dotted with bogs. Some of them have water in the center. Most of them today, after drainage, are covered clear across by thick, soft mosses. It is hard work to walk across a bog, since one sinks to above the ankles with almost each step. Many a cow has had to be rescued after sinking down to her belly in a bog. The bogs provided grass that was cut and stored for winter use. In addition to grass, the bogs produced **ängsull** ('meadow wool'), pors, cloudberries and small cranberries. One can understand then that the bogs were economic assets and became individually owned.

Not only the climate and the soil conditions are responsible for how the forest looks. Man has influenced these forests very much in the last three hundred years. Slash and burn methods, thinning of trees, clearing of fallen trees and bushes have been used since the Middle Ages to stimulate more grass to grow. Logging and reforestation and many a forest fire have changed the appearance continously. The iron smelters' need for charcoal, in particular in the southern part of the fäbod area, have devastated some forests. "It's a widely spread notion today," writes Montelius, "that there was an excess of grass in the forest in the old days. This is pure myth. The original forest, untouched by man, was literally a primaeval forest. There was no grazing, much less any grass to cut. The forest was either thick and dark with virtually no vegetation on the ground, or it was scrubby and bushy and covered by fallen trees in the process of rotting. Only after clearing with an axe or fire did man get grass for grazing and cutting. The grass in the forest then is to a very high degree a product of man, a product of culture."

DALARNA'S CLIMATE

The winter is long — almost six months long. The first snow can come in October or November, and spring snow storms may come as late as the end of April. Not only is the winter long, it is dark too. In the Lake Siljan area, the sun rises at 9:16 a.m. on December 20th and sets at 2:40 p.m. A person knows much of the year that tomorrow will be darker than today, and that knowledge makes man turn inward.

These conditions had an effect on the women. During the last weeks at the fäbod, when it was getting darker and darker, the women longed for the day they could return to the warmth and security of the village. Many of them surely felt, during these last weeks, that they didn't want to return to the fäbod next year. But almost all of them did—-and did with enthusiasm.

After the cold, dark winter months, each little sign of spring is observed with reverence, shared with others, and deeply enjoyed. There's a feeling of hope in the air and much anticipation. All through the winter, memories of last summer are hung on golden threads for the inner eye and only the positive, delightful things are remembered.

"And if it gets too wearisome during the winter, you understand, then I think about the summer and the fäbod, because up here it is so beautiful," explained Kersti. So when the spring sun starts shining and warming the earth, the women start to look longingly up towards the mountains and their fäbodar.

The summers in Dalarna are short (June, July, August) and intense with many daylight hours. They are seldom hot, but can have periods of 85° F weather. Some summers it can rain for weeks on end. But more than rain or sunshine, the light influences behavior. The sun rises at 2:27 a.m. on June 20th and sets at 9:36 p.m.

The long, summer evening's light had an effect on the mood, which contrasts sharply with the moods of winter. One can walk comfortably at midnight in an open area in the forest or up on the mountain slope and see for miles in a sort of hazy bluish light. It's like a long, out-stretched twilight, never getting completely dark all night long. The birds start singing at 2 a.m., exuberating energy. That and the light might be the reasons the women at the fäbod could put in such long working hours—often from 4 a.m. to 10 p.m. Not only did they work long hours, they also had a social life. One woman wrote, "I remember Saturday nights when the young people got together at the fäbod and danced . . . until the night's twilight was suddenly sliced by flaming, dazzling sunrays."

HOW DID THEY BEGIN?

Lars Reinton of Norway believes that the tradition of fäbodar came to Scandinavia from the east with the boat-axe people during the latter part of the Stone Age. These people were farmers, not wandering nomads, so for them the fäbod was secondary. By 800, the fäbod system in Norway was well established and moved from there with the Vikings to Iceland. They are described in the Icelandic sagas and in the Landna´ma´bok.

John Frödin argues that in some areas the earliest people were nomads who moved from place to place with their cattle, transporting their shelters with them. Later, they built a series of permanent sheds. Later yet, they started to break the ground along the river banks, which had the best soil and was easiest to clear. When these fields along the river banks were increased, it required that the family spend more time there and thus that place became the permanent home and the other sheds became fäbodar. In areas where this was the pattern of development, the fäbod was primary and the village secondary.

Sigurd Erixon disagrees with Frödin. Erixon sees the farming as primary and the use of the forest for hay as secondary. The people spent their summers, taking their cattle with them, migrating from one haying area to the next. As time passed, they built sturdier and better sheds to live in next to their hay meadows and bogs, and thus the fäbodar grew up.

Sigurd Montelius sees the fäbod development in Dalarna this way:
"The colonization went up along the river Dalälven and its tributaries where people homesteaded on the easily handled soils. The fields were small and poor and not even big enough for growing the needed grain. The cattle therefore had to seek summer food in the forest outside the village. There the people also cut grass from meadows, clearings, and bogs for winter use. The conditions stayed like that all the way up to the end of the 19th century. Through inheritance, the individual homes grew to villages. Daily feedings for cattle thus had to be found deeper and deeper in the forests and, finally, the cattle were taken so far from the village that they couldn't return at night. People then built a barn in the forest for the cattle and a simple cabin for the herder. Thus the fäbod was created."

Olle Veirulf points to extensive gathering of forest products other than hay as the creator of fäbodar in the northwestern part of Dalarna. The fäbodar were built as centers for fishing, hunting of beavers and otters, collecting birch bark, leaves, and mosses. In some instances, fäbodar were built next to where bog iron could be found, so the farmer could have milk products to eat and a place to live while the bog iron was collected and melted.

Much research remains to be done before the questions of why and how the fäbodar were built and what their original functions were will be answered. It is probable that the reasons and origins were different in different areas, and that's why we have so many conflicting theories.

THE OWNERSHIP OF THE FOREST

The ownership of the forest is a rather complicated matter. In the Middle Ages, the forest was considered no man's land. As long as the population was sparse, new homesteads could be built without any problems. But with the population growth came the necessity of dividing the forest and establishing borders. New rules and regulations were continually being added.

The first demands for dividing the areas seem to have been in connection with gathering birch bark or bog iron and establishing fishing rights. Later came the demands to establish borders for the grazing areas. By the end of the 17th century, a general segmentation of the forest seems to have been completed. Each county was divided into quarters and each quarter was given a section of the forest, held communally by all who owned land in the quarter.

The different herds grazed more or less at random within the section in the beginning, but as the population grew, the demands on the grazing increased. The result was arguments and soon it became evident that some kind of organization was needed. A complicated system of grazing routines grew up with borders like creeks or ridges keeping the different fäbod teams apart.

At the end of the 18th century, pressure increased on the grazing area and greatly expanded the fäbod system. Many arguments over grazing rights were settled in the district courts.

The forests nearest the settled areas were organized first, but as fäbodar were established deeper and deeper in the forests, they reached the area where no county borders had yet been drawn. In reality, the fäbodar drew the borders there first, and the counties later came to follow these lines, going zig-zag, following creeks, ridges, edges of bogs or shorelines.

MILK PRODUCTS WERE A MUST!

By looking at grain production statistics in Dalarna, one can understand the tremendous value of the milk products from the fäbod. The earliest fields were broken on the sedimentary soils along the rivers and there the villages grew up. The fields were small (approximately five acres per farm for the period 1570-1830). The yields were also small. Statistics for yearly production can be found and studied in records of tithes paid to the church. These records are not totally reliable, since a tendency not to record one's absolute income has always existed. Still, excessive cheating was unlikely, since the farmer paid tithes to the minister who himself was a farmer and not easily fooled. What causes problems in studying and comparing the statistics of crop yields is that the size of the measurements was not established exactly. A bushel of rye in 1570 might not be the same as a bushel in 1610.

Grain production in Leksand averaged 13.4 bushels per farm in the period, 1570-1572. By 1666-1675, it had increased to 15.4 bushels. For the ten year period, 1665-1675, this gave each adult male 1.87 bushels of grain per year to be used for bread, porridge, and beer. Seen in calories, it gave 2200 per day. The estimated calory need for heavy work, like a farmer's, is 4500 calories per day. By the mid-1700's, an average man in Leksand ate two bushels of grain a year, compared to about double that amount for a man in southern Sweden. When looking at grain statistics, one must bear in mind that one needs to work with averages. Some years had a larger crop, while others, with an early frost, for example, meant starvation.

The grains, barley and rye, were not the only crops grown. Potatoes were introduced into Sweden in the early 19th century. Before that date, a type of rutabaga was the main root crop. Even into the present century, the population of Dalarna lived mostly on bread and porridge, eating very little protein. During spring and summer, they could supplement their diet with fish. Salted herring could be bought throughout the year, depending on the cash available. In October, cattle were slaughtered and the meat salted down to keep as long as possible. Fresh meat was eaten during the holidays, at weddings, and at funerals.

These deficiencies in nutrition forced the people to rely upon the products of the fäbod. Milk products were treasured because they supplied most of the protein. Milk products supplied 15 to 25 percent of the total intake of calories. The cows then were one of the most valuable possessions; loss of a cow was a tragedy. Much more time was spent taking care of the cows and gathering winter food for them than was spent on the grainfields.

Cows at a summer fäböd

VARIATIONS

It is rather difficult for an outsider to grasp the degree to which villages and fäbodar not far apart differed socially and economically. But during my field trip in the summer of 1980, I found the people of Dalarna were very much aware of such differences. I often heard comments like, "In our area, nobody could afford a maid or a hired hand like they could over there." "Downriver some 15 miles, they have much larger fields and a more open environment. We have always been more crowded, so we had to develop more rules and pressures to conform." "We don't talk as much or as easily as them, so you can find more stories there. We mostly sang during evenings at the fäbod."

Frödin explains the differences between villages:

"In the old days with a lack of transportation, each community became a world of its own with economic organization and social traits being shaped by that area's specific natural resources and by that community's historical tradition. The type of organization varied thus from community to community, and since the fäbod was a link in this organization, they varied, too, in character and type to the same degree."

Since fäbodar grew out of an economic need, they adapted and modified to different and changing environments rather easily. If necessity is the father of invention, survival is the father of adjustment. The fäbodar, like villages, have displayed an ease of adjusting from the Middle Ages to the present.

Montelius explains:

"It is virtually impossible to describe the Swedish fäbod system completely and totally free from objections. Inside the rough frame, shaped by nature, technology, and economy, the fäbod system shows a large degree of variation from one time period to the next, from one area to the next, often close to each other. One meets a long line of variations and complicated combinations of different types and patterns."

Montelius also observes that the larger the village, the more complicated the fäbod system.

It is difficult to determine exactly how many fäbodar existed at different times. The eight counties surrounding Lake Siljan had about 240 fäbodar in 1663. Two hundred years later, that number had increased by 45 percent. At the end of the 19th century, an estimated 2000 fäbodar existed in Dalarna. In 1980, there were 178 fäbodar in use.

Fäbodar were scattered from nearby forests to mountain sites a day's journey away. One explanation for the great variation in distances to the fäbod can be seen in the example of the village Moje in Gagnef County. There the cows had always been taken to graze in the forest next to the village, but as the population increased, that forest was cut down and converted into fields. By that time, all nearby forests had been taken up by other villages for their fäbodar, so the people of Moje had to walk their cows across the valley and to the outlying forests at the south end of the county, which bordered on Grangärde.

As the population increased, new fäbodar were built and established ones grew larger. From approximately the middle of the 17th century, district courts granted permission to build new fäbodar. A group of farmers who wanted a fäbod would get together and locate an area in the forest they liked, then ask the court for permission. An appointed commissioner would check that the prospective fäbod didn't crowd already established ones, and if it didn't, the farmers could build theirs.

Through a rather complicated procedure, some farmers could get permission to "move in" on already established fäbodar and become part of that team. If grazing was already used to a maximum, the members of the team would vote against such a move and the farmer had to try some other method of getting a fäbod. If he had money, he could buy one or a part of one.

Inheritance practices in Dalarna complicated the ownership of the fäbodar. One farmer could own 1/8 of a cabin at one place and maybe 1/15 of a fäbod in another direction, or at its worst, he could own only part of a haying meadow. Through trading, swapping and adjusting, they managed to keep functioning. The government moved in during the 19th century and reorganized the entire ownership of land in Dalarna. This reorganization is called **Storskiftet** (The Big Redistribution).

THE BIG REDISTRIBUTION

In spite of laws against it, the people of Dalarna continued their old inheritance practices. Each child inherited his or her portion of each bit of land, buildings, fäbod, meadow, and bog, which the parents had owned. Towards the end of the 18th century, the splintering had gotten so bad that rationally functioning farming could not take place. Before the Big Redistribution, Larspers Lars Persson of Djura, one of the worst examples, owned 212 pieces of land in 65 different locations. Björk Anders Andersson of Djurabyn owned 369 different pieces of land. Some of these pieces were no wider than six yards. Not only was it difficult to work such small strips of fields, but also there was a great loss of time, walking from one piece to the next. This was true in particular for haying meadows and bogs in the forest. The families would spend days, walking to and from these in the middle of the summer.

By federal law, this reorganization of ownership of land took place county by county. This process began in 1802 and wasn't completed until 1894. All the maps drawn in connection with the inventory done before the Redistribution could take place are a rich resource for the study of the size and location of each fäbod.

Some of the aims of the Big Redistribution were to give the farmer preferably one fäbod instead of parts of several fäbodar at different locations and to give those farmers that didn't have one an opportunity, through trading off land, to get a fäbod.

The farmers that had been moving their cows between two or three fäbodar each summer stayed mostly at one fäbod throughout the summer after the Redistribution. Of course, the Redistribution was not done in the same manner from county to county, since the farmers were a large part of the deciding force.

If a farmer did not have a fäbod before the Redistribution, he could lend his cows out to a fäbod for the summer. As pay, the owner of the fäbod received part of the milk products. Some areas had better grazing and could take in these "borrowed" cows. As long as there was enough feed, it worked, but county after county made rules against this practice as the forest became more and more crowded.

NAMES TELL A STORY

While names of fäbodar is a fascinating folklore topic, big enough for a separate research project, I will do no more than barely touch the surface. When, for instance, I first saw the name 'Backbuan' (**backe**=hill; **buan**=dialect for 'fäbod'), I thought Backbuan had gotten the name from its location on a hill, but that is not the case. When surveying the ownership of that fäbod, I discovered that the farmer who built it came from the village of Backen.

Other examples of villages giving their names to fäbodar: Lindbuan from Lindbyn; Tjärnbuan from Tjärna; Stenarvsbuan got its name from the village, Stenarvet, which has been gone since the early 1700's.

Names of mountains (**berg**) were sometimes given to fäbodar: Bastberget was named after the giant, Basten.

Lakes also gave their names to fäbodar: Ösjöbuan from Ösjön (**Ö**=island; **sjö**=lake); Tansbuan from the lake, Tansen, named after the giant, Tansen; Skällbodarna from Lake Skällen.

The name of the farmer who built or owned the fäbod can be seen in many instances: Eriksbodarna, Matsbodarna, Olhansbuan, Svensbuan, Jansolarsbuan, Brömsbodarna, Erikhansbodarna, and Ollarsbodarna.

Events seem also to have given names to fäbodar: Middagsbodarna (**middag**=dinner or supper); Brandskogsbodarna (**brand**=burned; **skog**=forest); Trätbodarna (**träta**=to argue); Myggbodarna (**mygg**=mosquito, a name my son wanted to give to every fäbod we visited).

Some fäbod names derive from descriptions of the surroundings: Risåsbodarna (**ris**=twigs or brushwood, **ås**=ridge), Torrbergsbodarna (**torr**=dry, **berg**=mountain); Granbergsbuan (**gran**=spruce); Ängsbodarna (**äng**=meadow).

CHAPTER TWO

THE BUILDINGS AT THE FÄBOD

The buildings at a fäbod illustrate the people's frugality, practicality, and their adaptation to geographical conditions. A simple but very sturdy log cabin was built for the vallkulla to live in. The cabin was small enough to heat, but large enough to move in with ease. The furnishings were purely functional, often serving more than one purpose; a bench in day time, for example, became a bed at night. When some fitting or furnishing was needed for the cabin, locally available materials were used; a hook on the wall, for example, would be fashioned from a naturally grown "hook" in a small tree or a suitable fork in the branches. Such hooks were also used in the villages, but they were abandoned there in favor of carved or lathed hooks much earlier than at the fäbod. The milk-house, placed close to the cabin to save the vallkulla steps, was built of the thickest lumber to keep the insides as cool as possible. The farmer was, at times, concerned with comfort and aesthetic beauty, but when it came to the buildings at the fäbod, functional utility was his primary index of choices.

Even the choice of a location for the fäbod illustrates their practical adaptation to the geography and economic conditions. One of the most important factors in the choice of a location in the terrain for a fäbod was the availability of water. Not only did the cows need water to drink, but the vallkullor needed a lot of it every day for washing the utensils. Verna Smids at Lindorna fäbod reports that she carried about

120 gallons a day in 1976. The close proximity to springs, creeks, or lakes was therefore of utmost concern.

Terrains known to keep the snow late were avoided—for example, low-lying areas facing north or marshy flats. Mountain slopes facing south or southwest were treasured as sites for the fäbod, since they were warmer and free from late spring frosts. These slopes often had sufficient ground water to keep the grass growing thickly and to encourage a more varied type of flora.

Frödin mentions in his study of Orsa that the contact with the home village determined the choice of location to some degree. If a fäbod was placed high up on the mountainside, the women had "a free view home, and thus didn't feel so lonely." This type of location had a practical aspect also. The vallkulla could, in case of an emergency, blow a signal on her long wooden horn and be heard all the way down to the village.

Montelius points out a common misconception,

> "that most fäbodar are located on mountains high above their surroundings, the so called top-fäbodar. But many other types exist: plateau, hill slope, lake, bog, etc. Within the larger fäbod complexes, one finds a combination of terrain types. It is virtually impossibile to make a classification of the types of terrain locations chosen for the fäbodar."

Many fäbodar do have fantastic views of the valleys, lakes, and mountains. As many an old vallkulla has said, "The mountains look bluer from up here." To see the sun setting late at night beyond the western mountain and experience the stillness of the vast expanse, undoubtedly influenced the women that spent their summers at the fäbod. For some, it offered a closer contact with the world, a sort of melting together with nature, while others got a religious feeling. "One is closer to God up there." This, of course, wasn't the aim in choosing the spot for the fäbod, but the result.

LAYOUT OF THE BUILDINGS

Seldom was a fäbod owned by one isolated farm unit. Instead, it was common that several farmers got together, cleared a suitable location, and helped each other build their units. A typical unit consists of a cabin, a milk-house, a small barn, hay-loft, cooking shed, and corrals adjoining the barn. A couple of small meadows surrounded these buildings. A fäbod settlement could range anywhere from a couple of these units, up toward 30 or 40. Bastberget in Gagnef, one of the largest, had about 55 units in the latter half of the 19th century. How the different units were located in relationship to each other was totally determined by the terrain. Each unit was fenced in and separated from the others by a lane. These lanes, called **fägattu** 'cattle lanes', were used by the animals when they walked to and from the

Interior and exterior of an eldhus.

forest.

Each fenced-in unit had a cabin as its nucleus, where the vallkulla lived. Next to it, or adjoining it, would be the milk-house. The barn was located nearby and placed to serve two purposes: it should be close to the lane, and have a dung opening facing the meadow, so that the dung didn't have to be transported long distances to the meadow. The door of the barn was at the gable end, facing a small, fenced corral, which opened onto the cattle lane. After the cows had been milked in the mornings, they were kept in this corral until all the other teams' cows were ready and they could all be taken to the forest at once. They were also kept in this yard when they returned in the late afternoon until the vallkulla was ready to let them into the barn to be milked. Sick or pregnant cows were kept in the corrals all day long.

The dung from the barn was thrown out through an opening in the wall opposite the door. The dung hill grew right under the hole in the wall and was distributed across the meadow in the fall by the men.

"People talk of how romantic a vallkulla's life was," commented Edit Niss in an interview at Ösjöbuan in Gagnef. "When I had to walk across the dung heap with some big old shoes on to stamp it down because it had gotten so high we couldn't throw out any more, I didn't think it was one bit romantic."

THE ELDHUS, OR HEARTH CABIN

The **eldhus** 'hearth cabin' was the most primitive of the cabins used for living quarters; they were definitely much simpler than contemporary houses in the villages. The hearth cabin is a one-room log building with the door and often a breeze-way at the gable end. The dirt floor is usually 10-15 inches below ground level and was sometimes covered by spruce bark or branches. Some have stone slabs on the floor, particularly near the door. The hearth cabin does not have a proper fireplace with a chimney, but a simple open hearth. Stones are placed on the floor in a circle or a rectangle, and the fire is kept inside the stones. The smoke finds its way out through a smoke hole in the roof. Either there is an opening along the entire ridge of the roof with one side of the roof ending short of the center, while the other side extends a few feet over the ridge to keep out the rain, or the smoke escapes from a hole built on the same principle right over the fire.

There are no windows in the hearth cabin, only a small hole in each wall. These holes are called "wind eyes" in some areas. (Note the similarity to Old Norse "vind auga," the source of the English word, "window.") The holes could be closed by a clump of moss, a plug, or a sliding lid. While sleeping in a hearth cabin, I found that if I had the holes open, lots of mosquitos came in and kept me awake. If I closed the holes, the room soon filled with smoke, since less drifted out the roof's smokehole, and that kept me awake, too. Nothing in fäbod

Sketch of eldhus interior.

folklore adapted to mosquitos.

The cabin has wide benches on three sides. These could be resting on rocks or short logs made to fit, or all three could be attached to the walls. Sometimes, the two long ones rested on a short bench, which was attached to the walls and resting on the rocks. The benches were made of thick boards or half logs with the flattened side up.

Some cabins had wide benches against the walls and a narrow bench further out in the room below them. The women slept on the wide, side benches along the walls, with their heads against the gable wall, or they slept on the shorter gable bench and used the longer ones for storage and for eating. The narrow benches were used for sitting and the wide bench was used as a backrest. During the haying season, every bench was used for sleeping.

The cast iron cooking pots hung from two parallel poles extended across the room from above the door to the other gable wall. Across these poles were laid shorter poles. Chains of wood or metal were hooked onto them. The wooden hangers had a naturally grown hook at the top, which hooked over the cross bar. At the bottom was another hook where the cooking pot could hang. It could be raised or lowered by adjusting plugs in holes.

The roof was built of natural hooks and thinner poles which were attached to the rafters in such a way as to hold the rectangular pieces of birch bark which were placed on top of the rafters, starting from the bottom and each higher course overlapping. The layer of bark was covered by split logs, placed with the round side out. These were kept from sliding off by an eve-board placed inside the hooks.

The birch bark lasted for about 40-60 years and then had to be replaced. Bark was gathered in June or July, often during the days when the families were cutting the grass on the bogs. The bark was peeled off in approximately one-foot-wide strips. They were laid on the ground in stacks, insides to insides, and rocks were placed on the stacks to flatten the bark. Man-made materials like tar paper and tile replaced bark in the roofs in the villages, but since nobody would carry those heavy materials to the fäbod, the bark roof remained in use there long after it had disappeared in the village.

A hearth cabin at Sten was used until 1953. One of the vallkullor who once lived there describes it:

> "We slept farthest from the door on the side wall bench. We had hay under the skin rug, linen sheets, and quilts. Spruce bark that had been peeled during the sapping period in the spring was placed below the bed area to be stepped on like a rug. We were supposed to pour water on the dirt floor and stamp on it till it got smooth and beautiful. We put a small birch tree by the bed each Saturday and spruce branches along the walls in the breezeway and in the milk-house, and it smelled so good. The breezeway was a kind of parlor where we hung clean towels. We picked wildflowers and put them in a bottle there."

There isn't much light in a hearth cabin. Some comes through the "wind eyes" in the walls, while most comes from the smoke hole in the roof. The fire created a lot of smoke that coated the inside walls with soot. Knis Karl Aronsson's father, Knis Aron Karlsson, told his son the following story:

> "About 1890, I came into a hearth cabin at Älgbergsbodarna where the vallkulla was cooking meat. A calf had broken a leg, and she had been forced to slaughter it. The woman stood by the fire with her sleeves rolled up. She had blood up to her elbows and soot in her face. The cabin was black from soot, with just a stream of light coming down through the smoke hole. It was a picture of pagan savagery."

Hearth cabins standing today can be found only in Ore and Älvdalen Counties. Such cabins once existed as far south as Leksand County, according to Knis Karl, but they are all gone now.

Carl von Linne relates seeing hearth cabins in villages on his travels through Dalarna in 1734. Sigurd Erixon believes that these cabins were used on the farms as summer living quarters in the Middle Ages, while other scholars believe that they were used year round in the villages.

When a house in the village was being replaced by a new, bigger, and more modern one, the old house was often taken down and the logs numbered in sequence. The logs were then transported by sled over the snow to the fäbod, where it was later reassembled. One proof of this tradition is a house at Ärteråsen. The year a house was built was generally carved into the log right over the door. The house at Ärteråsen has 1662 carved over the door. We know that Ärteråsen was not established as a fäbod in 1685, since it was not included in that year's inventory. The first time Ärteråsen is mentioned is in a border argument in 1770. Many of the buildings at this fäbod show carved dates from the 1730's, and it is logical to assume the fäbod was established then. Thus it appears that the house with the date 1662 carved over the door was moved to Ärteråsen and rebuilt there.

If one wants to study the architecture of 16th and 17th century villages, he can go to the fäbod and find the buildings. If the original buildings no longer exist, one can find copies of the old buildings, for the inclination toward praticality and simplicity often made the farmers rely on earlier styles at the fäbod, long after they were building more modern homes in the villages.

THE CABINS

The other cabins used for living quarters are usually younger than the hearth cabins. It is impossible to set any kind of general date for them, since there is a great deal of variation within the area.

One-room cabins are very common. They were built of peeled spruce or pine logs, flattened or concave-convexed on sides that were

The construction of a birch bark roof.

25

touching. The corners are the so-called Scandinavian type: the logs are notched on the top of the log, or on both the top and bottom, before being joined **(knuttimrade)**. The ends of the logs extend a uniform distance beyond the corner of the building. Most cabins were left unpainted, but some were painted with a bright red paint that was produced cheaply as a by-product at a copper mine in central Dalarna. These cabins typically also had a rough unpainted plank floor, small windows, and an open hearth fireplace with a chimney in the corner. In later years, cabins were built with an entry hall and a room for storing the milk products. These cabins vary considerably in layout and furnishings.

The cabins most closely resembling the hearth cabin had a door at the gable end and a fireplace in that corner. A cast iron pot could be swung in over the fire by an arm which was attached to a pole going from the floor to the roof. The beds were nailed to the walls. Some of these cabins had only openings for windows, while others had windows. Before the days of glass windows, the linings of pigs' stomachs or cauls were used.

One cabin was very common. Typically, it sat upon a rock foundation and had stairs leading to the door, which was placed on the long side of the building. One entered a small entry hall first, where hooks held outdoor clothing. The main room had an open hearth in the corner, beds along the walls and a table in the corner or by the window. Some of the tables were hinged to the wall, using naturally grown loops of juniper as hinges. This type of table could be used as a shutter to close the window at night. Open shelves along the walls stored the few utensils needed for cooking and eating. Benches nailed to the wall and a couple of stools solved the seating arrangements.

Some women saw the fireplace as an object that could be made artistically beautiful. The first week at the fäbod each year, they would whitewash it. Some also put on borderline decorations.

But the artistic impulse most evident in the fäbod area expressed itself in a rather peculiar tradition. One bed was made up in the most elaborate fashion and never slept in. Here the vallkulla's best hand work was displayed. The top sheet was folded down some 15-20 inches over the blanket and this section of sheet was richly embroidered or filled with laces. The pillow case was often much longer than the pillow, draping over the edge of the bed and displaying one lace after another. Anna Bäckström said that crocheted or bobbin laces belonged to her mother's generation, while plainer patterns, mostly embroidery or cross-stitching, belonged to her grandmother's. But for both of them, the habit of making the bed as tight and flat as a parlor floor was important.

The storeroom for the milk products had a tight fitting door that closed it off from the living quarters. It had no windows, only a small air vent facing north. The logs were thick and tightly fitted together, and that kept the room cool. This room was cleaned and scrubbed down when the fäbod was opened for the summer and kept immaculately clean throughout the summer to protect the milk products.

THE MILK-HOUSE

If there was no separate room in the cabin for storing the milk products, there would be a milk-house nearby, often joined to the cabin by a breezeway. Some milk-houses were dug halfway into the ground, while in later years others were built over a creek.

The milk trays rested on a 'milk ladder,' which consisted of pegs fastened to the walls. A series of shelves suspended on four ropes from the ceiling was used for storing cheeses. Other shelves could be nailed or attached to the walls with pegs, all in accordance with the changing needs.

To keep the milk-house clean and fresh, the vallkulla scrubbed the walls and shelves often and used the materials they had available to them at the fäbod. Birch bark or scrubbed stone slabs would be used to cover the shelves. Chopped juniper or spruce branches were strewn on the floor and placed in any available nook or corner to make the room smell fresh.

BARNS, SHEDS, FENCES

The barns were small, windowless log buildings with a wood or dirt floor and individual stalls for the cows. Barns without stalls also existed, in which case the cows would be tied to the wall at certain intervals. The cows were tied to the walls with metal chains and hooks, or earlier with withes made of birch branches. The goats were kept in a goat pen or left to wander loose in the barn. Edit Niss related, "We had a goat that just couldn't fall asleep unless she lay next to her favorite cow."

To keep out mosquitos and gnats, the barn door was kept closed and the dung opening was closed with a lid.

The barns opened onto a common lot or onto individual corrals which were used alternating years.

The hay lofts were log buildings with a dirt or wood floor and a simple roof. The shape and size adjusted to the circumstances. One, for example, was placed across the border between two meadows. It had a door at each end and a dividing wall in the middle, so that two owners could share it. Another barn had only one door, but was divided lengthwise.

Many of these log buildings that once dotted the forests have now rotted, since they were not needed after hay started to be grown in the villages at the beginning of the century.

The 'gaping sheds' and 'haying sheds' (**gapskjul** and **slogbod**) were the most primitive sleeping quarters in the fäbod complex. They were used only during the haying period and were located near the bogs or meadows, way off in the forest. Basically, they were low sheds with three sides and a sloping roof, capable of keeping the rains out and some of the mosquitos off. The latter was accomplished by a fire built at the opening end; the smoke it created kept the bugs at a distance (sort of). The people slept on a bed of spruce branches with their feet toward the fire.

One of the things one identifies with rural Dalarna is a specific type of fence, called **gärdsgård**, made of young pine and spruce saplings, tied together on a slant. They can now be seen even in towns, but they were originally a forest product.

Pine or spruce poles about 1 1/2 yards long are sunk in the ground in pairs about 4 inches apart with a yard between pairs. Each pair should lean slightly apart. The slanted scaffold poles are from 3 to 5 yards long, the bindings are made of spruce, juniper or birch branches, or spruce bark strips.

VAGABOND'S DIARY

Everybody carried a carving knife. There's a Dalarna proverb that expresses the value of that tool to a man from Dalarna: "A nobleman without money is as worthless as a farmer without a knife." Free time was often spent whittling or carving designs. Many of the wooden tools illustrate the carving skills that seem to have been rather common. Not only the men carved, but the women at the fäbodar did too. The doors, walls, benches, and furniture are covered by many a vallkullor's initials, owner's marks, dates, proverbs, short poems, and thoughts. Visitors to the fäbod also carved their messages.

Many visitors wrote in the soot on the walls of the hearth cabins, but their messages are gone now, having been sacrificed on the altar of 20th century cleanliness. These soot writings, according to reports, were longer and more elaborate than the carved ones. One vallkulla commented, "At the end of the summer, we would read in the soot which boys had been visiting, and we were very careful not to wash it away."

The carvings remain today and can be studied. The most common carvings seem to have been initials and dates. If the initials end with "S," they belong to a man — a son (Andersson). If they end with a "D," they are a woman's — a daughter (Andersdotter).

Owner's marks are also very common. Not every owner's mark signifies that that family once owned the fäbod. They were often used together with the initials, or in lieu of them. The only carving one can accept historically is the date carved into the log right over the door— the year the cabin was built. Some excelled more than others in carving on the walls. Some carved initials, while others carved short lines about the work, fatigue, loneliness, homesickness, the weather, as well as lines about happy times and fun.

"I carve my name with honor and not shame. K A D 1827"
"B A D Here I stand so worried 1848"
"I P D The first year I herd 93 all is well"
"I say farewell this year last Monday of the summer."
"E A D Easy to be here but I am homesick 1844"
"Now I have got my fill of herding Anna Sturk 07"
"A S E D B P D are good friends at work at Ärteråsen"
"A J D I have many faults but God knows them all"
The boys visiting Saturday nights added theirs:
"G G S and A M D 1734 Let us be merry"
"Petters I H S this I have carved a Sunday.
"Good to be here 1885"

Erotic jingles can be found, but they lose their rimes and puns in translation:
"Lars 1747
In Norboda awake the whole night longing for a pussy."
(I Norboda hela nat har jag vaka efter fitan jag raka)

One rainy day during haying, one man carved
"Here are three lazy men at Åsen one had snow-socks the other heavy shoes I'm A E S doing absolutely nothing today it rains too much I don't dare go outside."

In Karl Linell's hearth cabin in Linaasen, one can read the following carvings:
"Look at the fool in Sunahe 1828"
"Look at the one eating 50 potatoes"
"I wish to leave this boring world."

On another wall, at Gisselbo, two girls expressed their feelings:
"The world is so dark and heavy if one doesn't get any free men while young"
Pictures, mostly stick figures, can also be found. On the door at Linåsen, someone carved a figure with pointed fingers and claws on the feet and wrote "the devil" under it. The Swedish word for devil is 'fan'; someone later changed that word to 'far,' which is the word for 'father.'

One poem carved on the inside of a bed expresses the feeling of a Sunday morning:
Here among pleasures from surroundings
We enjoyed lovemaking
And what we did, nobody knows
Except the bed, she, and I
(Här bland nöjen utav tingen
njötos kärlekens behag
och vad vi gjorde det vet ingen
utom sängen hon och jag)

Montelius, who has visited virtually every fäbod in Dalarna, writes that nowhere in Dalarna had he seen such rich and varied examples of carvings as at the fäbodar in Ore County. "Most of them are skillfully made. One gets the impression that the vallkullor and visitors competed in carving as beautifully as possible."

Björn Hallerdt has studied some remarkable carvings in a hay loft at Ärteråsen fäbod in Ore County. Three men from Skattungbyn, a village in Orsa County, carved their initials, P E S 1697, I M S 1697, and I I S 1703, and their villages' names, then went on to carve a series of elaborate hunting scenes. Hallerdt writes:

"The carvings show men and animals. Most men carry weapons on the hunting trail. Many of them have dogs along, and some of them are riding horses. The weapons are carefully carved and exaggerated in size. Even the hunted animal is so clearly carved than one can identify the species. The clothing, even if simplified, offers a very interesting study. In particular, three items have been carved more carefully: the hat, the jacket, and the pants. The hat is round-topped with wide upturned brim. The jacket reaches to the hips, has a belt around the waist and a couple of seams on the front. . . . . The pants give the clue to which period the costumes belong. . . . . It is the Baroque's adventurous warriors that meet us here in a farmers' copy, fifty years late."

Samples of the carvings Björn Hallerdt studied in a hay-loft at Ärteraasens fäbod. These pictures, drawn by Gunvor Hallerdt from pencil rubbings, do not show the varying depths of the carvings, nor their intricate shadow effects. (Dalarnas Hembygdsbok, p.54).

CHAPTER THREE

WOODEN TOOLS, FOOD, UTENSILS

Most of the tools and utensils used at the fäbod reflect the same conservativism, frugality, and utility as the style of the buildings. When new tools or utensils were acquired in the village, the old tools were usually taken up to the fäbod and used there for several more years. For an old man to come up the fäbod and use 'that old wooden spoon . carved so many years ago' must have had a strong emotional impact. For the vallkulla, who used metal utensils in the village, to come each summer to the fäbod and use the same wooden milk trays and buckets that grandmother had used must have felt reassuring. The tools at the fäbod had a way of tying the generations together.

Wooden tools and utensils were used until the beginning of this century when metal utensils gradually became available. Plastic came after World War II.

It has generally been believed that every farmer made his own wooden utensils as they were needed by his household, but this is wrong, says Rosander. "Even to get simple items, many a farmer asked a talented neighbor for help. Some wood items were made solely by specialists, since they required trade skills and specialized tools." Rosander goes on to say,

"For many of the tools and parts of tools, naturally grown cores were used, not carved. Each man always kept an eye out for trees or branches that would be suitable for boatsides, skis, hollowed-out bowls, hayforks, handles, etc. These cores were taken home as they were found and put aside if they were not needed at once.

"Birch wood was most commonly used for harnesses and tools, as well as for bowls, spoons, and ladles. This wood is hard and heavy and does not easily crack. For furniture, stave containers, sieves, bushels, etc., pine was used, or sometimes spruce.

". . . Juniper was used for butter tubs, drinking cups, and the large buttermilk containers. Ash wood was used for teeth in rakes, as well as bird-cherry wood and maple, since these woods are hard. Aspen and apple wood were also used."

ARTISTIC EXPRESSION IN WOODEN TOOLS

Folk artifacts often display two things: they are functional at the same time as they are artistically pleasing. A round or oval butter dish is easier to carry in a back pack than a square one, whose corners make it hard to pack and may hurt one's back. Rounded butter dishes were also easier for the vallkullor to clean. A milk tray had an aesthetically pleasing, flowing shape, while, at the same time, the wide surface made it easier to skim the cream off. The sieve serves well the need to strain the milk and, at the same time, it is beautiful with its sloping sides and soft curves. Some tools are also admirable in their use of locally available materials, for example, the scrub brush.

Artistic imagination and skill flourished on the bottoms of the cheese molds. The cheese was pressed into the mold and turned over after a day, so that the design was impressed on two sides of the cheese. Many of these molds had the owner's mark carved in the bottom, so that the vallkulla could keep the cheeses apart when she took care of cows for more than one family.

TOOLS USED FOR CLEANING

Cleaning brushes, brooms, and detergents are the items that show best how the vallkullor adapted to the primitive conditions and did what they could with what they had. Many brushes were needed to scrub all the milk trays, bowls, churns, cheese molds, etc. The women picked a plant called 'horsetail' and tied it into bundles, which worked well as scrub brushes. When one wore out, they didn't have to walk far to get material for another one. They also cut off the tips of spruce branches and tied them into whisks. A large number of these had to be made and dried so that the needles fell off. These were then brought home to the village and used throughout the winter. **Skäfte**, a grass which contains silicon, was also tied into bundles and used for scrubbing utensils.

Detergents were not used at the fäbod until very late. As a substitute for detergents, the vallkullor chopped juniper branches and berries, which they boiled in water. The liquid was then poured into the container they wanted to clean and let sit for a few hours. Sand, preferably fine-ground, quartz-rich sand, was used as a scouring agent. Anna Ericsson-Hayton describes how they scrubbed the floor an early Sunday morning:

> "To clean the floor, several buckets of water were carried from the creek and half the floor drenched with cold water. Sand was spread over the floorboards. Two of the young women began the scrubbing, which was done by putting two flat spruce brushes on the wet floor. The girls stood side by side, one foot on the brush and their hands on each other's shoulder, and rubbed as hard as they could, so the sand hissed around their naked feet and the sweat dripped from their faces. When two floorboards were done, another girl came and rinsed them with a lot of clear water to get rid of the sand. Then she would come with a scraper made of several layers of birch bark stuck in a piece of wood. With this tool, she scraped off most of the water."

The big cast iron pots were cleaned the first day at the fäbod with boiling water and ashes, but, after that, sand was used. The vallkullor scrubbed the insides of these pots until they shone as if they were made of silver.

TOOLS USED FOR MILK PRODUCTS

The women milked into a **stäva**, a bucket built on the stave principle. From this container, the milk was poured into a storage container through a sieve or strainer. The sieves varied considerably. In the western and southern parts, a wooden sieve was placed across the storage container and a filter placed inside. The filter was made from cow, horse, or human hair, which had been spun and sewn into a circle. The women from Vamhus often walked from farm to farm, making these filters, called **siltapp**, from material each housewife had collected. These straining tools were not carried along with the goats during the haying trips. Instead, a bark cone filled with small juniper branches was made each day.

The milk was stored in trays until the cream had surfaced so it could be taken off. It was skimmed off simply by holding the tray in the right hand, while the left hand acted as a breaker for the cream, while the milk was slowly poured into another container. The cream was then scraped off both hand and tray into the butterchurn.

The butterchurns vary a great deal. One family could have two or more churns to be used according to the amount of cream on hand. Very few churns had lids.

The butter was gathered from the churn and put in a bowl, where it

Butter dishes built on the stave principle, held together with birch withes.

was worked with cold water and a large wooden spoon. "It was a real trick to roll it, at the end, just right, so it formed a beehive looking cone," explained Ida Hane. "Some women just put the butter in containers, but I never did. Grandma was always so careful to form the butter into a beautiful cone, and I did the same."

The cheese molds consisted of four walls (usually 10" x 6" x 5") and a bottom that could be removed in most instances. In the bottom, a groove was carved, so that the whey could run off as the cheese was pressed in.

THE MILK PRODUCTS

The vallkullor's main task at the fäbod was to produce as much cheese, butter, and whey-butter as possible. These products were carried home to the farm and stored there in the cold cellars for winter use. Butter was sometimes sold to provide a cash income.

By far the most important fäbod product was cheese. If a vallkulla tended more than three cows, she made cheese every morning. "To get the cheese tasting really good, I put in cummin seeds," said Liss Anna. "I know some people didn't, but I mixed the goat milk in with the cow milk when I made cheese. That cheese had a very special rich taste that we liked on our farm."

After the turn of the century, rennet, the substance that curdles milk, could be bought in the store. Before that time, rennet was made at home. When a farmer slaughtered a calf that had eaten only milk, he saved the rennet bag. This bag and its contents were rinsed carefully, salted heavily, pinned shut with small sticks, and hung up to dry. When rennet was needed, the bag was soaked in water for a couple of hours and then hung up to dry again. If stronger rennet was needed, a bit of the rennet bag could be put directly in the milk.

This is how Edit Niss described the way she made cheese:

"Each morning, I had about four buckets of milk, which I let set until I skimmed the cream off. I poured the skimmed milk and any buttermilk I had on hand into the big cast iron pot and added the rennet. I heated this and took it off the fire before I walked my cows to the forest.

"When I got back an hour later, I stirred it well with a big wooden ladle and let it settle to the bottom, while I went out to the barn and cleaned it and made it ready for the cows to come back. That done, I would slip down and take a dip in the creek. When I got back to the cabin, I lifted the cheese-curd up and pressed it really hard into the cheese molds and put them in the store room.

"The next day, I would turn the cheese over in the mold. After that, I took the cheeses up and stored them on the shelves, turning them every day so they would dry right.

"There are several things one has to be careful about. If the milk was too hot when the rennet was added, the cheese would be dry and hard. If the whey was not pressed out properly, the cheese could sour, but if too much was pressed out, the cheese got dry."

In some fäbodar, a "big cheese" was made over a period of several days. Many small cheeses were saved, kept damp, and stirred into the newly curdled milk. When this settled, it was packed into a special, big cheese mold. This cheese was left to ripen in the farm cellar and taken out to be eaten during a holiday.

One cheese in particular, "the little cheese," is connected with fäbod traditions. The vallkulla gave this cheese away during the festivities the first days after she returned to the village in the fall. These days will be described in detail in the chapter on courting and festive activities.

The whey that remained after the cheese was taken out of the cast iron pot was used for making whey-butter. Edit tells how she made it:

"About every three days, I cooked whey-butter. I'd pour all the whey into my biggest cast iron pot, which held 25 gallons. I had to start early in the day, since it took 7-8 hours to cook.

Thank goodness, I didn't have to chop the firewood myself. My father and brothers did that. When the whey had come to a boil, I skimmed the foam off, and then it would settle down to a slow boil. The first few hours, I didn't have to watch it too closely, other than keeping the fire going evenly. When it had boiled so long that it became yellowish, I had to stand there stirring it all the time, otherwise it would burn. After the whey-butter was finished, I let the fire die down and the whey-butter cool off."

(Here, her sister, Ida, interrupted and told that she used to add a bit of sugar, flour, and anise at this point, because it made the whey-butter thicker and tastier.)

"It was very important that I didn't touch the pot while it cooled down, because if it was shook, the whey-butter became grainy and grandma didn't like that at all. Many a vallkulla tip-toed around, not to shake her cooling whey-butter. After it had cooled, I put it in a container in the milk-house."

The two sisters sat, reminiscing how good that real home-made whey-butter tasted. "Oh, in the winter, to put butter on a rye-crisp and sprinkle the top with whey-butter that had gotten so hard we had grated it— that was the best tasting ever."

If all of the bits of cheese were not removed from the whey, the quality of the whey-butter was low. This was nicknamed "lazy whey-butter." Burned whey-butter was called "fiance whey-butter," alluding to the vallkulla thinking about her lover so she forgot to stir her whey.

All milk was left to stand until the cream could be skimmed off and saved. The vallkulla made butter once or twice a week. There are many little secrets about how to make the best butter. Edit got up at 2 a.m. while everything was still cool. "If you did it in the heat of the day, it just turned into a gravy. It was so embarrassing when that happened!" Other vallkullor sat in the cool of the breezeway, churning in the early part of the day, while some dropped in a silver coin to make the cream turn quickly into butter. Many wanted the cream slightly sour, to make the butter taste really good.

The foam that forms on the cream just before it turns into butter was eaten if there were guests in the cabin. This foam, served on rye bread, was considered a delicacy. An old saying, undoubtedly started by some frugal housewife, held that if men ate too much of this butterfoam, they would get very horny; so the vallkullor were teasingly tight with their foam.

The butter was scooped out of the butter churn into a wooden tray, where it was worked through, or kneaded, with very cold water. After that, it was packed into wooden containers and stored.

How often the milk products were brought down to the village depended on the distance between fäbod and home. The ones the furthest away never got any visitors from home, except during those weeks in July when the haying was done. Then the men carried the products back to the village with them. Closer fäbodar would have their products fetched more often.

UTENSILS FOR COOKING AND EATING

The **kräkla**, made from the top of a young pine tree which is cut off just below the first set of strong branches, is a very practical tool. The branches are cut off about three inches from the stem and the bark peeled off. It is used for stirring porridge as it boils, gravies, and whey-butter; it is especially nice for making whey-butter smooth after it has cooled down. If a **kräkla** broke, it wasn't difficult for a vallkulla to make herself a new one.

Wooden spoons were carved for eating. Each vallkulla had a spoon of her own, marked in some way with a design so nobody would mix them up. They were not stored in a drawer, but hung in a rack on the wall. These spoons were commonly in use at the fäbod longer than in the village, where metal spoons began to be used after the turn of the century.

The author holding a kräkla.

Before wooden plates made on lathes became common, people ate out of one big serving bowl, or dipped their bread into it.

"Eating from a communal porridge bowl entailed its own special technique and etiquette. One had to help oneself in a considerate manner in one's own sector of the bowl, not encroach on the neighbor's territory, nor sneak too much of the central butter pat. If milk was served with the porridge, one was not supposed to slosh it around and make the bowl unappetizing for the others. The spoon for porridge eating was short-handled and held vertically when dipped into the bowl and then put into the mouth, narrow end first. The handle on this type of spoon was shaped accordingly, with a well-defined thumb grip."

Coffee was a much-appreciated luxury for the vallkullor. A **gnurka** was used for grinding the coffee beans. It was carved from one piece of wood and a rolling mallet made to fit. Coffee was boiled in a three-legged copper pot, standing all day in the corner of the open hearth.

NO FANCY COOKING

Åsa Nyman writes in her article about fäbod food,

"The weekly chores, the demanding work making butter and cheese at night, left hardly any time or strength for fancy cooking. Meals were not regular; the vallkullor ate when they found the opportunity. The limited raw materials and the simple way of life, which often demanded food of the packed-lunch type, contributed to preserving ancient standards of cooking, which go back to a primitive housekeeping based on cattle-farming and the need to store products for the winter."

The food supply carried from the village usually consisted of bread, flour, dried meat or salted herring, coffee, sugar and salt, and sometimes potatoes. There seems to have been very little variation in this list, until the beginning of this century, when the standard of living rose.

Edit Niss explained that the first years she worked as a vallkulla, she ate only porridge and milk products. When her mother came up to visit and brought some pork, her stomach ached because she was so unused to meat.

"In later years, Liss Anna, Britta, and I took turns cooking dinner one day each. We put salted pork or lamb in a pot and boiled it for a couple of hours with potatoes. The next day, we ate the leftovers as a soup. Some days, we fried salted herring. Liss Anna was very good at making pancakes for dinner."

A variety of dishes were cooked with rye and barley flour (wheat flour was not common until around 1910– 1920). Porridge was cooked with flour and water, buttermilk, skimmed milk, or whey. Lots of gruel was also cooked. **Välling**, a dish of hot milk thickened with flour, was very popular. **Sull**, rye-crisp or hard-tack crumbs soaked in milk, was a quick meal to fix.

A variety of dishes utilizing whey-butter were often prepared at the fäbod. "One could put whey-butter shavings on top of rye crisp, porridge, or sour milk. Or one could pulverize dried whey-butter and boil it in water or milk, making a gravy into which bread was dipped."

Tradition held that when visitors came to the fäbod, they were to be treated to the best of foods, and the vallkullor used what they had at hand. Many dishes utilizing fresh milk, whipping cream, and fresh cheese were invented. One of these was the foam from butter-making, as mentioned earlier. Newly made butter, not yet salted, was considered another treat. So was cheese made from whole milk, and porridge cooked with cream. The crust that formed on whey-butter as it cooled could be skimmed off and made into a dough with flour and cream, then rolled into buns and boiled in whey.

Stirred cheese (**rör-ost**) was made by not removing the cheese-curd from the whey once it had settled, then heating it, stirring constantly, until it looked like porridge. With a bit of sugar added, it became a delicacy.

Skillet cheese was yet another dish which shows that you do what you can with what you have. When no oven was to be had, a deep cast iron skillet was used. Whole milk and rennet were cooked to a thick consistency and poured into the skillet, where it was slowly fried.

Tjesfil was yet another invention to please the guests. The vallkullor often poured milk and cream directly into the eating bowl and added rennet. This turned out to be a frothy dish, nicknamed "blowing wind" in some areas.

"You know," Edit concluded, "that when we have a coffee party down in the village, we are supposed to serve seven different kinds of cookies. Well, here at the fäbod, we did that too. All we had here were dry rusks, so we said as we served them, 'Be sure to taste all the seven different cookies.'"

BACKPACKS AND HERDING BAGS

The vallkulla carried three bags with her on days when she herded all day long. The back pack was made of birch bark strips. In it, she carried her lunch and fire-making kit. On one hip hung a bag filled with **sletje** (flour, salt, chaff or hay mixture for the cows). On the other hip hung a bag which contained the shirt or the embroidery the vallkulla was working on while the cows rested for lunch. The vallkullor all knitted while they walked. Some invented a kind of hook that they hung from their belt or waistband, to which they attached the ball of yarn, so they didn't have to stop knitting to pull out more thread from the yarnball in the bag.

TOOLS FROM BIRCH BRANCHES

Thin, peeled birch branches, called withes, were used as hinges, hoops on stave containers, strings, etc., and were made into chains hung around the cows' necks and used as tethers for tying them to the stalls. At the fäbod, chains made of withes were in use much later than in the village, where metal replaced the wood. As part of her workload, the vallkulla had to make a specified number of chains from birch branches or twigs each summer.

To make withes, the thin birch branches and shoots were cut in the early part of the summer and the bark peeled off. A few vallkullor peeled with their teeth. "It was rather easy to do—but poor teeth and lips! One hadn't stripped the bark off many branches before one's mouth was very sore." The chains were made either by twisting two withes together or by taking one long one and making loops in it.

The vallkullor also made the brooms, whisks, and brushes used at the fäbod, as well as a large supply needed on the farm through the winter. The whisks were made of thin, peeled twigs tied into bundles. Brooms were made of unpeeled birch branches tied into bundles. In some areas, the vallkullor made a special broom to celebrate Midsummer. The leaves were left on this one, since fresh green birch branches were used in every possible way to decorate everything from the Maypole to the cabin.

HOW VALLKULLOR TOLD TIME

It may be surprising that the vallkullor were concerned with keeping time, considering the rather primitive conditions they lived under. That it was important one can understand from the many reports from all areas of having to have the cows ready to leave for the forest at 6 a.m., or 6:30, or 7, sharp. It was considered shameful to be late and make the other vallkullor wait until the slowpoke got her cows ready. Maybe it was more difficult to live without an alarm clock than without a watch. "There was once a girl that had such a hard time waking up in the mornings that she stuffed her bed full of wooden trays and bowls. She was so uncomfortable that she woke up easily." Often, it turned out that the woman who had "an inner alarm clock" and woke up by herself took on the responsibility and woke the others up.

There were several methods of telling time during the day.

"The animals should be ready to be let out at 6 o'clock, or earlier in the morning. Under no circumstances were they allowed to stay inside until 7 o'clock. We had no alarm clocks.

Lines representing the different hours were carved on the floor. As the sun progressed, the shade from the window or the opened door showed what time it was as it hit these lines. To know when it was time to walk home in the late afternoon, the vallkulla looked at the pupils of the goats' eyes. When the light diminished, the pupils got larger."

Some vallkullor knew how to read time by the length of their shadows, while others looked at the sun's position in relation to some mountain or cliff.

FLINT AND TINDER

Even if matches could be bought and were used in the village, the typical vallkulla, out of frugality, used a tinder box. In a leather pouch, she kept a bit of steel, flint, and tinder. The steel and flint were bought from wandering peddlers. The tinder was made from porous mushrooms that grow on birch trees. The outer layer of the mushroom was cut off; the rest was boiled, dried, and pounded to a fibrous pulp. To start a fire, the vallkulla would hold the flint with the left hand's thumb and index finger and the tinder in the fingers just below it. With the steel in the other hand, she would strike the flint, knocking sparks into the tinder and lighting a fire.

OWNER'S MARK

Each household had a mark, a specific design, that was put on their possessions. It is a brand, in a way, but a brand is connected with cattle, while in Dalarna it had a much wider usage. It was used in lieu of a signature on legal papers and sales agreements; it was carved onto the bottoms of wooden utensils, and onto the handles of tools, sewn into shirts and bedding, knitted into socks and mittens, carved into wooden chests and furniture, and scratched onto cowbells, keys, locks, and hinges. Not surprisingly, people carved their marks for fun into trees along the trails and at resting spots during the herding, or scratched them into rocks.

The use of **bomärken** goes back to the period prior to the Viking Age, according to Mats Rehnberg in his article "Bomärken." In 1347, a court ruling recognized their legality. Since that time, they have been used on weapons, seals, official documents, and gravestones, as well as on personal possessions.

The use of **bomärken** persisted in Dalarna later than in any other province of Sweden, and later there in the rural communities than in the cities. After general education was established in 1848, the tradition of **bomärken** began to fade out, but some areas kept it up until this century. A limited use of them is reported from Sollerön as late as 1938.

Bomärken from Gagnef. The top two rows are made from rubbings off wooden utensils at the museum. The bottom four rows are copies of bomärken recorded at Gagnef's county commissioners' office.

The **bomärke** was used by several generations and thus became the mark of the farm, rather than of an individual. The son that didn't inherit the farm, but built a new one, often used his father's mark as a base and added a line or two to it. If a son-in-law took over the farm, he did not use his family's mark, but that of his bride's. If a farm was sold, the new owner did not use the seller's mark, but made up a new one. In some areas, the **bomärken** were entered into an official log book.

Up at the fäbod, the **bomärken** had several functions. They were carved over the door of the cabins; this was never done on the houses in the villages. Carved on tools, the **bomärke** also settled arguments about who owned an item. All the tools that were stored over the winter could easily be separated when the fäbod was opened in the spring. The **bomärke** could also help in recovering stolen items. "Someone had stolen the quilt we had at the fäbod. When my husband came in one day in the winter to the cabin of a logger, he saw our quilt. He had only to point to the bomärke, and the man gave it back."

In case the vallkulla was caring for cows belonging to several farmers and poured all the milk together, she used the **bomärken** to keep a record of the amounts of milk for each owner. For each farmer she would make a long stick and carve his **bomärke** on it. With a small stick, she would measure the depth of the milk each time and record it with an incision on the long stick. At the end of the summer, each farmer would have a set of long sticks, on which the amount of his milk for each day was recorded in a long line. The milk products were then divided according to the total length and the proportions. The vallkulla could also keep the cheeses apart by the **bomärke** imprinted on the cheeses. She carved small flat sticks with the owner's mark on them and stuck them into the whey-butter and butter to keep their ownership straight.

CHAPTER FOUR

THE COWS:
GRAZING, HERDING, AND HAYING

Until about the end of the 19th century, farmers in Dalarna kept more cows than they were really able to feed; their cattle were usually at the starvation point. Since the Middle Ages, the aim had been to keep as many cows as possible alive over the winter. When spring came, many a cow was too weak to walk out of the barn unassisted. Some even had to be carried out. If spring was late, it could bring severe difficulties. Most years, the winter feed of grass and hay was suplemented with leaves, mosses, chaffs, and bark in varying amounts, depending upon how the season before had been. In October, the farmer would check his supply of fodder and then estimate how many cows he could keep alive over the winter. The rest, most often the calves, he would slaughter. The aim, then, was not to get as much milk through the winter as possible, since starving cows deliver very little, but to keep them alive for the fäbod visit, when they would produce better. Montelius has pointed out that there was another important reason for keeping as many cows as possible:

"Without cows there would be no manure, without manure no grain harvest, and without grain no food supply. It was the availability of manure that determined how much grain could be grown . . . . The people of Dalarna were caught in a vicious circle from which they couldn't break loose until modern technology solved the fertilizing problem. As the winter wore on, milk production decreased while the manure heaps outside the barns grew and predicted the size of the harvest from the barley fields. When I was a child, the old people told me how they, as they walked to church, surveyed and commented upon the different farms' dung heaps. It was a taxpayer's directory of sorts. When domineering parents looked for a suitable marriage partner for their children, the size of the manure pile was a guideline."

Some old fäbod barns where larger doors had to be cut also indicate that today's cows are bigger. One can also go into a fäbod barn and see how very crowded the cows are today. Each one takes up a much greater proportion of the space than their predecessors.

It follows that when the cows were that much smaller they also produced less. It's very hard to find any statistics on milk production until this century. It is estimated that a cow in 1571 produced 35-50 pounds of butter per year and weighed 100-140 pounds when slaughtered. A cow of today produces 340-360 pounds of butter per year.

There seems to have been a local preference as far as the breed of cows were concerned. In the region bordering the timberline, the white Alpine breed dominated. The women there felt they were the best; they ate less than other breeds, gave richer milk, and they were more musical. "They listen at once when we start to sing, not just the cows but the calves too, and they follow us as soon as we start to walk, singing. The 'red cows' don't do that; they just keep on eating."

Around Lake Siljan, the "red cow" breed was liked most. The women said that they were the most intelligent, manageable, alert, and independent-thinking. The bell-cow of this breed kept her herd together and she took her role with dignity. There are lots of stories told of how faithful, kind, and wonderful these cows are. The bell cow even kept an eye on the calves and kept them in line. One story told how the bell-cow, after discovering that the calves had been left behind one morning, walked back to the fäbod on her own and got the calves.

What is important here is not which breed was used (this varied considerably through time; besides, the cows were often not of one breed, but a mixture of several). What is important is the relationship between the women and their cows. Many a cow was treated like a member of the family. One of the reasons for this, of course, is that families depended on the cows to a very high degree for their existence. Since it was only the women that milked and herded, the women and the cows spent a lot of time together. Tranquility might best describe this relationship.

One of the expressions of this closeness to the cows can be seen in the choice of names for the cows. Very often, the calf was given the name of a beautiful thing or image—Twinkle, Silver-flax, Dove, Lily,

Star, Rose, Dazzle. Another reason for choosing a name is the wishful transference of a quality. For example, **gås** is dialect for butter; many a cow was given a name compounded with **-gås** to express the wish that the cow would produce an abundance of butter—Flower-gås, Beauty-gås, Star-gås, Lots-of-gås. The cows could also be given names referring to their coloring or design or a mark in their hide—Blacky, Redstripe. Or their names could refer to the day they were born—Saturday-Star, Friday-gås.

Goat names were more mundane than the names of cows. The goats were treated collectively, often with frustration. They were known for disobeying and causing a lot of irritation. If a stranger came to milk a goat and she wouldn't let the milk down, that person could wear the clothes of the person who usually did the milking and so beguile the goat into giving her milk.

ALL-DAY HERDING

The vallkullor followed their herds of cows and goats all day long, virtually to the end of the 19th century. This was done for three reasons: to protect the animals from wolves and bears; to ration the available supply of grass and help the animals find the best grass; and to keep the animals off neighbors' land and off areas intended for haying.

Wolves and bears were a part of everyday life in Dalarna well into the 19th century. Twenty-three bears were killed in the last big hunt near Venjan in 1856. During the 20 years between 1834 and 1853, bears and wolves killed 410 cows, 135 heifers, 35 bulls, 14 horses, and 8 colts in Leksand County alone. During the five-year period, 1866-1870, 100 bears, 21 wolves, 96 lynx, and 1 wolverine were shot in the whole province. The last wolf was killed in 1916, and today a few bears still live near the Norwegian border. Logging was begun on a large scale in the last part of the 19th century and is a main reason for the beasts' disappearance. The loggers shot some; the rest of the animals migrated to other areas when men began working in the forest.

For the vallkullor, these beasts were a constant problem. Generation after generation heard stories of brave vallkullor protecting their herd, or fighting with the bears over a cow, calf, or goat. Since the cows held such a valued position in the family's economy, and since the vallkulla was responsible for their lives, she could not run for protection if a wolf or bear came near her herd. Anna Bäckström said the vall kullor "were more concerned for their cows than themselves."

If a vallkulla discovered a wolf or bear nearby, she would bang an axe on a tree, hoping the bear would think loggers were nearby, or she would make as awful a noise as she could to scare the beast off, or if she had a fire going, she would throw a burning branch at the animal. Some went after the bears with pokers. One vallkulla told of how a bear was pulling her calf away and she got so mad she grabbed the calf, pulling it in the opposite direction. When the bear still didn't let go, she grew furious and slapped him across the face with her bonnet. He was so surprised, he let go and ran off.

Per Johannes's grandma (born 1827) told how a bear had come close and scared her animals the summer she was 12 years old. She had been taught not to run away, and the only thing she could think of doing was to sing a hymn as loud as she could. The surprised bear turned around and lumbered off.

Almost every vallkulla carried a signal horn as long as the threat from the beasts was imminent. The horn came either from a cow or a billy goat. The cow horn had from three to five holes drilled in the side, so that a melody could be blown on it. Each melody was a message which everyone was familiar with. The billy goat horn had no holes drilled in it and was used mainly to scare off wild animals, since it was believed that beasts hated its harsh, penetrating sound.

Another instrument, too cumbersome to carry along while herding, was used around the fäbod to scare off the bears and wolves. It was the lur, a wooden horn about one-and-a-half yards long. Only the most skillful of vallkulla could get a melody out of this instrument, so it was used mostly as a noise-maker. These instruments and their uses will be discussed in detail in the chapter on music.

There was yet another method of making the bears turn around and wander off, and it is an example of the vallkullor's adaptation to 'do what you can with what you have.' During the largest part of the 19th century, the women at the fäbod did not wear any underwear. They wore ankle-long skirts, but no panties. A vallkulla could shame the bear into turning away and walking off by turning her back to the animal and pulling her skirt over her head, giving him "the cheeks."

The vallkulla herded to ration the limited amount of grass available as effectively as possible, while helping the cows to find the best grazing areas. "The cows do have an uncanny knack for going right back to the area they just ate off," explained one vallkulla with a sigh.

In order to ration the grass supply, an intricate rotating system developed. This organization is an example of how the fäbod system adapted to the situation. Each fäbod settlement was allotted a seg-ment of the forest, called a löt. If a fäbod settlement consisted of five grazing teams, the löt was divided into five parts. These parts were in turn divided into segments, called gässlor (gässla, pl. gässlor), which were grazed off one after the other. When the last had been used, they started over again with the first. Many vallkullor did not fol-low this routine exactly, but let the grass supply and the weather decide to some extent which gässla she chose for the day.

Each gässla had a carefully chosen spot where the cows lay down to rest and chew their cuds for a couple of hours in the middle of the day. This spot was called the sovhol (sov=sleep, hol=place). It was often located on a knoll, by a stream, or on a peninsula sticking out into a bog, or it was surrounded by tall spruce trees, giving shade and acting as a borderline.

When it was time for the cows to rest, the vallkulla would blow a melody on her horn or sing it, and the cows, knowing the melody, came. The vallkulla started a small fire. To keep the mosquitos and gnats away, she put wet moss or damp branches on the fire. This would produce enough smoke to at least hamper the bugs. Then the vallkulla ate her lunch and worked on her sewing. Very often, the vallkulla would run over to visit at a nearby **sovhol**.

The uses of some **sovhol** were so intricately designed that oral messages and news could be sent from the village up to the vallkulla or back—a type of jungle telegram. A person in the village would go up to the nearest **sovhol** on a set day and start a message to the vallkulla. The next day, that first vallkulla would meet another to whom she gave the message. She in turn met the next vallkulla at her **sovhol** the next day, and so on until the message had worked itself up the mountain to whomever it was intended for. In his article, "Folklig Telegraphering," Erixon mentions that, in order to get messages across lakes, two vallkullor would stand on each shore on a specified day, hollering across to each other. "Messages and news could be sent thus between Nybodarna and Katilla, a distance of 36 miles. This took a week."

Another reason for herding all day was to keep the cows and goats from eating grass that belonged to somebody else. It was also expected that the vallkulla would carefully check that her animals did not graze on the meadows and bogs which were saved for cutting as winter fodder.

When herding all day no longer was needed, the women walked the cows to an area they had selected for the day, leaving the animals there and then walking back to the fäbod. The cows usually walked home by themselves in the afternoon, or they were called home by the vallkulla singing her message to them.

Anna Bäckström, who spent her summers at the fäbod as a child in the 1920's and worked as a vallkulla into the 1940's, explained how they divided the grazing.

"We were two teams, one at the upper end of the fäbod settlement, one at the lower. Both teams sent their cows out to four different gässlor and kept rotating these round and round all summer. It never happened that we collided and sent them to the same place. I don't know how it functioned; it just did, because we had always done it so."

WHEN A COW GOT LOST

It is very important that a cow is milked twice a day. If a cow with a young calf goes much longer than 24 hours without being milked, she dries up. Other cows can go for as much as 50-60 hours. It was therefore a serious problem if a cow wandered off from the herd. If one judges from the stories told about lost cows, it was a constant concern for the valkulla, in particular during the late summer and early fall when the mushrooms started to grow. The cows loved to eat the mushrooms and could wander far in search of them. Betty Andersson remembers,

"I can still see Mother as she tied a scarf around her heard with a determined gesture, lifted my baby sister up on her arm, and walked off into the forest that dark September evening to search for the cows. My other sister and I both had to walk along, as we were too young to be left alone in the cabin.

"Mother worked her way through the forest, found a cow-trail she could follow a stretch, then walked up on a hill, stopped, listened, and called. Never will I forget Mother's melodic, strong herding calls. But the forest stood quiet. We just had to go on. Mother shifted the baby from one arm to the other while the darkness increased, and Mother's worry and fears rose until we suddenly heard that well-known tone of our lead cow's bell. Sure, it was still very distant, but we knew we would find them, and we rejoiced.

"During the walk back, the moon shone on the small group of people and animals that returned home, tired and quiet. I remember I thought the moon smiled scornfully. The baby had fallen asleep in Mother's arms.

"Adventures like this didn't happen once, but many times."

During the years the vallkullor herded, it could happen that a cow wandered off in the middle of the day. The vallkulla would blow the "My cow is lost" signal on her horn. The sound carried over miles and other vullkullor could hear it. They, in turn, would blow the appropriate melody, perhaps "Look no more; I've found your cow." But with the discontinuation of daily herding, the number of vallkullor out in the forest diminished and the vallkulla had to depend more on herself for the first couple of hours of search.

If a cow was lost, the group collectively supported and helped out. The women that stayed at the fäbod filled in and did the work for the ones who went out searching through the forest. As long as they could avoid it, the vallkullor did not ask for help from the village in their search. A question of honor was involved. A vallkulla had accepted the responsibility for the cows, and she would naturally be reluctant to let it be known outside her group at the fäbod that she had failed in her assignment. But if the cow or cows could not be found within a day, a message was sent to the village and one man from each farm that had a part in the fäbod would come up and organize a big search.

CUTTING HAY ON MEADOWS AND BOGS

One of the reasons for establishing fäbodar was the gathering of hay in the forest for use as winter fodder. The whole farm family worked for weeks each year, cutting, drying, and transporting this winter fodder. Because the shortage of grass was an ever present threat, each straw was important. "Grandma used to walk across the newly cut meadow, ripping off each blade of grass left around the rocks or tree stumps, collecting them in her apron," said Anna Bäckström. "After the haying, the meadows looked like they had been shaved."

An inscription on the bottom of a milk tray says, "1782 I was here in Mackmyra fäbod from June 26 until August 4 and harvested not one straw. God knows what will become of us this year."

In 1937, Hall Anna Mattson told John Granlund: "The last time they cut the grass on the bogs at Flenarna fäbod, five persons worked for two days, and they only got one small stack. Grandpa's brother-in-law got so mad he emigrated to America."

Grass was cut at several types of places through the forest: on bogs, along lake shores, on meadows, in clearings, and in the cleared meadows surrounding the fäbod. From a woman's description of her youth in the 1860's, Montelius has figured out that one family in Järna walked 150 miles each summer, from one haying area to the next.

The time haying began varied with the climate, as is reflected in two old proverbs. "When the heather starts to bloom, it's time to cut the hay." "If you see one ear of barley in the valley, walk to the bogs, but if you see three, run."

THE HAYING

Gustav Dalmalm remembers haying around the turn of the century:
"We were up and started by 4 a.m., cutting the grass while it was still damp from the dew. At 7, we ate a breakfast of potatoes and herring, a dish that tasted delicious after the early morning work. After breakfast, we took a little nap and they started the cutting again. We ate dinner at noon sharp. By then, it was hot from the sun and the grass was so dry that no scythe would cut it, and besides, we were rather tired by then. We enjoyed the dinner of pea soup and sandwiches. Then followed a couple of hours of quiet around the haying area when everybody took a nap in the hay lofts. In the

afternoon, we raked and stacked the grass that had been drying in the sun. If one was really keen on working, one could cut some more in the evening, when the grass had gotten damp again, but usually one was quite happy to go to bed instead for a few short hours of sleep in the hay loft."

The tools used were the scythe, the rake, the pitchfork, and a drying rack called a **hässja**.

The shape of haying scythes varied somewhat, depending upon region and personal preference. Scythes in the southern parts had short, straight handles with one or two grips; in the northern parts, they tended to have longer handles with a cured end and only one grip. A handle was most often made by the man who used it and made to fit his height—it should be as long as from the ground to his arm-pit and the grip should sit where his clenched fist touched. The same scythe was used for all tyeps of terrain, with the exception of very rocky meadows, where an old, sawed-off scythe would be used so it would be easier to cut close to the rocks.

A **hässja** frame. All but the bottom cross poles are removed and hay hung across it. Another cross pole is added as each succeeding rank is filled.

Women did most of the raking. They used a special rake, which was shorter and lighter than the men's. The rakes were made of birch. The 21 teeth were carved with a knife, attached with tar in the holes drilled with a thin drill and enlarged with a heated iron, which made the holes conical.

When the hay had dried, it was taken to the hay loft. If it was left on a **hässja**, a fence had to be made around it to keep the animals off. Usually, the tops of pine trees with the branches left on were laid around the **hässja**. The hay was hauled home to the village on sleds after the snow had fallen. Every member of a fäbod team had to drive up the same day, in order to help each other making tracks and shoveling when the snow got too deep.

No date can be set for when haying was discontinued on the bogs and forest meadows, since it depended on the amount of hay grown in the valleys after modern methods and fertilization came in. Cutting the bogs generally ceased during the first decades of the 20th century; later, other areas were successfully left uncut. The last haying on bogs may have been that in 1960 at Skallbygge fäbod in Ore County.

HAYING—A SOCIAL TIME

The vallkulla looked forward to the one or two weeks the haying people would be in the close vicinity of the fäbod. It meant more work for her, cooking for the large group of people, but it also meant company from several villages. A lot of visiting went on—practical jokes, story swapping, and dancing in the evenings.

A fäbod west of Lake Siljan

"The biggest fäbod weekend was the one around July 12 when people from the villages cut the grass. They spiffed up the best dress they had brought along and cooked special festive party dishes. That weekend, there were parties at all the fäbodar. Everyone that could play brought his instrument, so we played a lot of games and danced."

Karin Andersson wrote down her memories of haying days at the fäbod:

"Even if I live to be a hundred years old, I'll never forget how much fun we had. We used to all be in the hearth cabin, playing. If a boy had done some practical joke to a vallkulla, she often walked up to him and flirted. She had soot in her hand and, when she got cozy with the boy, she'd smear soot all over his face, and a wild chase would begin.

"We invented lots of other fun and games. Even the older people couldn't keep still, but took part in the practical jokes. If somebody had brought a fiddle, we would dance in the meadows, way into the night. Even the older and more sensible danced, too. Old waltzes and polkas were the best-liked dances."

WHEN FODDER WAS SCARCE

Since a shortage of food for the animals existed into this century, the vallkullor had to gather a variety of supplementary foods—leaves from birch, willow, alder, aspen, and mountain ash; mosses; even branches of spruce and pine.

The leaves of the mountain ash were picked one by one, since to strip the branches would have hurt next year's buds. Other trees were stripped: one's right hand was either left uncovered or covered by a glove or by finger tubes on the index and middle fingers. The base of the branch was placed between these two fingers and the branch pulled through. One started with the branches one could reach, then bent the rest down with a stick that had a naturally grown hook at the end. Sometimes, one would finally climb up into a tree and throw stripped leaves down to the ground.

The leaves were gathered into apron-bags, boxes made of wood shavings, or birchbark backpacks. A more drastic method was sometimes used: the vallkulla took off her long skirt, tied it at the waist and used it as a bag. The leaves were dried in hay lofts and brought down to the villages, together with the grass during the winter.

Mosses were used as a supplementary food north of Lake Siljan during years of severe grass shortage. Icelandic lichen was gathered while wet from rain (it would crumble if gathered dry). In emergency situations, it was cooked in water and given to the cows. During years of severe starvation, people ate Icelandic lichen also. The moss was brought home, dried, and ground to a flour. This was cooked with porridge, or baked into a loaf. This bread was nourishing, but black and bitter. The mosses of the sphagnum group were gathered with rakes and given to the animals, mixed with the grasses.

The bark off different trees was also used to ward off starvation, for bark is rich in vitamin C and sugar. The goats were fed the finer parts of spruce and juniper branches, as well as branches of deciduous trees which had been gathered during the summer by the vallkullor. The cows were fed spruce and pine branches in emergencies. During periods of starvation, young pine trees were stripped of their inner sheet-like bark, which was dried, threshed, and ground into a flour. Before being baked into loaves, the flour had to be leached to remove the pine-pitch taste. Many people are still living who heard their parents talk about that detested bark bread.

CHAPTER FIVE

THE MOVE UP TO THE FÄBOD

The day the people moved the cattle to the fäbod was like a much anticipated holiday. "We children waited with eagerness and impatience for the **buföring** (the move to the fäbod)," said Betty Andersson. "It was the *big* day of the summer. Several days before the **buföring**, you could feel it in the air. Excitement was everywhere."

Unless the cows had been let out of the barn for a few weeks to eat what green leaves they could find, they were too weak to walk to the fäbod. The first day the cows walked out of the barn, a variety of protective rites were performed. Some let the cows out on a specific day, often April 30, while others let the animals out according to the weather — if spring came early, they were let out about the middle of April.

The move to the fäbod couldn't take place just any day of the week. A tradition common to the entire fäbod area was that no **buföring** could be done on a Thursday. Randa, the lady of the forest, or the vittra-people (forest spirits), or the trolls were doing their **buföring** on Thursdays, and people had better stay out of their way. In some areas, farmers would not do their **buföring** on a day "back to back" with Christmas — that is, if Christmas Day came on a Monday, its back to back" day was a Monday. Äppelbo village did its **buföring** only on Tuesdays and Fridays, since the trolls were out the other days. In some areas, the **buföring** was done on Mondays, since dances were held for the vallkullor on the Saturday and Sunday evenings before leaving. In other areas, Wednesday and Saturday were considered lucky days for the **buföring**.

The days before the **buföring** were filled with activities. It was too far to walk home if something was forgotten, so the farmer and his wife were busy packing and re-checking. Into the wagon were stuffed tools, utensils, clothes, yarn and materials for shirts, some bedding and food—barley and rye flour, bread, dried meat, herring, salt, potatoes, and coffee. "When the wagon was loaded, the farmer placed a bag or two filled with hay on the very top," explained Anna Bäckström in a fäbod lecture. "There the smallest children would ride backwards, so that they had a view of the whole wide world as they rode up toward the mountains."

What time of day the march began on **buföring** morning depended of course on how many miles there were to travel. The people of the village, Nusnäs, who had their fäbodar at Krackelbacken, had 48 miles to walk. That was one of the longest distances. Eight to twenty miles seem to have been rather common. A cow can walk 12-18 miles per day; so, for some, it meant a stay overnight en route, either sleeping under the stars, or in some friend's fäbod along the way.

Albert Viksten remembers his childhood on a **buföring** morning. Though too young to join in the dancing, he had spent the night walking around.

> "The spring birds had gotten there. The songthrush had been singing all night and a sparrow greeted the new day with its very special song, ending with a beautiful flute sigh. The mystique of that bluish summer night penetrated everything. When the sun rose above the mountain, I heard them getting up at my home. It was about three in the morning. The boats were coming from the other side of the lake, where they had been dancing all night. They laughed and sang as they rowed home. It would be melancholy and empty after the vallkullor had left for the fäbod."

Then followed a few hours of bedlam. Last minute packing and re-stuffing was done. The cows and goats felt what was going on, and they ran around very excited, bellowing. The cowbells and goatbells rang, people hollered and argued, children chased animals or each other.

When everything was ready, the vallkulla would start walking, either singing her herding songs, or blowing them on a cow horn. The excited animals that ran ahead of her had to be caught by the children and brought back; mischievous goats had to be kept out of the farm fields along the way. The wagon would come behind them all. At the edge of the village, they would meet and mix with others going to the same fäbod. After a few hours of walking, the excitement would calm down.

Sometimes, the men took a separate route with the wagons, following the road, while the women and cattle took a short cut over the hills. They all met at the point where they had to leave the road and begin walking the trails. Here the wagons were unloaded and the horses' backpacks and saddlebags were filled. Sometimes, a travois would be used.

The trails leading up to the fäbod were often no wider than a couple of feet. Slowly, a single line of women, children, cows, goats, men, and horses would wander through dark spruce forests, over dry hard pine moors, through birch groves, and over wet bogs. And if there were rivers or lakes to cross, another bedlam broke loose. If a ferry was available, the animals had to be herded onto it and ferried across. The goats were the least cooperative. If there was no ferry, the cows had to swim. The vallkulla would take the bell off the lead cow and sit in a row boat, ringing the bell. The cows would then swim after the boat. The goats had to be rowed across to the other side.

Almost everybody knew the route to the fäbod, having walked it since childhood, but there were some local methods of marking the trails. In Leksand's forest, a stone placed on top of a tree stump pointed out the route to Skeppssjöbodarna, while a stone on top of a stone identified the trail to Digerbodarna.

All fäbod trails had specific places where travellers rested. Every such place had a name, either describing some natural phenomenon such as the view, or it was named for a person, or an event that had taken place just there. One resting spot, called **Vilstenarna** "resting stones," was marked by three stones of a chair's height, side by side. **Gammelvilar-lågen** "old people's resting place" was identified by an old moss-covered pine tree flat on the ground. **Hälftenstenarna** "half-way stones" were flat stones, half way between home and the fäbod. **Annas fläskbränna** "Anna's porkburn" was a spot where a vallkulla had stopped to fry some pork, but had started a big forest fire instead. **Krogen** "the saloon" was a resting spot by a creek known for its tasty water. **Filhällan** "buttermilk spill" was a flat rock where a farm hand had slipped and spilled all the buttermilk he was carrying. **Brännvin-slågen** "aquavit resting spot" (aquavit is a strong liquor made from potatoes) marks where some boys on their way to the fäbod for a Saturday night had dropped their bottle and broke it. It was considered bad luck to pass that place without offering a symbolic shot of aquavit—a green branch or a twig from a blueberry bush.

The cows knew that they were on the way to the fäbod and they knew the trail. Many vallkullor told of how the cows got excited, started to bellow and run when they came to the last stretch of the trail. Some cows ran and flocked at the barn, while others ran around and around. Anna Bäckström had one cow that ran each year to one particular ant hill and dug it up with her horns, spraying the contents high up in the air. After that, she didn't touch an ant hill the rest of the summer.

If the animals were excited at arriving at the fäbod, so were the people. "The cows were so happy when they arrived at the fäbod," explained Edit. "And we were, too!" added Ida. "The first thing we did was take off our shoes and socks and stick our aching feet in the cool creek. Then we put on the coffee pot."

Quickly, they had to turn to a lot of hard work that had to be done at once. The women cleaned the milk-house first, scrubbing it down with sand and juniper water. All the wooden trays, buckets, and butter churns were placed in the nearest creek to swell and seal any cracks. Stones were placed inside them, or on top, to keep them under water; this process was called "stoning." The women boiled juniper branches in water and poured the liquid into the vessels after they were taken out of the creek; many vallkullor said that was the secret to getting wooden utensils to smell good.

After the milk-house was cleaned, the food and utensils were unpacked and stored in there. Protective rites for the cows were performed, the cabin and barn cleaned, bedding aired, new hay stuffed into the mattresses, repairs done, spruce branches put in the milk-house, cows milked, and supper fixed. That first supper at the fäbod was like a party. Fresh milk was used in cooking the porridge, which was considered a treat. "And then," wrote Albert Viksten, "there was laughter, and practical jokes, wit and playful combat."

The men had several chores that had to be done before they could return to the village: repair cabins, barns, fences, or gates if needed, clear grazing areas in the forest from fallen trees, if that hadn't been done prior to the **buföring**, check bridges along the grazing trails, gather and chop spruce and juniper branches, and, above all, chop enough wood for the summer or until the next visit; shame on the man who let his vallkulla chop her own wood! Some men also gathered mosses for the cows to sleep on in the barn.

After the men had completed their chores, they walked back to the village, leaving the vallkullor to settle into a routine for a summer of hard work and long hours, but also a certain amount of personal freedom which they didn't have in the village community.

CHAPTER SIX

HOW DID THEY DO IT?

How were the women able to live isolated at the fäbod? How did they become so capable of acting independently? How did they learn to deal so resourcefully with a variety of problems? To answer such questions, we must know something about their personality and how it was formed. The isolation at the fäbod was a source of tension, at the same time as it brought the women of varying ages closer together; the vast forest was a threat if one lost her way, at the same time as it was greatly appreciated for its beauty and serenity; the wolves and bears were a source of fear, at the same time as they called forth the courage to deal with fear; the translucent summer nights made the vallkulla's work day very long, at the same time as the beauty transmitted energy to the vallkulla; the primitive living conditions were uncomfortable, to say the least, at the same time as they called forth the ability to make do with what one had and improve on one's lot.

Dalarna is a culturally conservative area. We have already seen how the people cling to relics of past material culture; they also cling to relics of past social and psychological traditions. Farmers in Dalarna have never been serfs under a feudal system. They have always owned their land and been their own master, never bowing down to anyone. There's an old proverb up there, "The oak tree and the nobility don't appear north of the river Dalälven." The people are proud of their traditions and are determined to keep them.

This independence and self-reliance has helped to shape the women of Dalarna, as well as the men. Since the 17th century, Dalarna has been overpopulated and the food shortage has forced the people to invent outside incomes. Women have provided a significant segment of the family's support. For their contributions, they were greatly appreciated and respected. This process made the women of Dalarna resourceful, strong, more independent and self reliant, compared to those wives who performed only household duties and who, as a consequence, were subserviant to their husbands.

OUTSIDE INCOME

The outside income came basically from two kinds of activities: making and selling handcrafts and seasonal work outside the province.

In many areas, during the 18th century, handcrafts became specialized. One area, for example, concentrated on barrels and, through time and experience, perfected the crafts so that they could mass produce them on a small scale. Mora became known for its clocks, Malung for its skin products, Venjan and Älvdalen for their containers made of wooden staves, and Leksand and Rättvik for their dalmålningar, peasant wall paintings. Basket making and items made of human hair from Vamhus developed a century later, during the 19th century. Weaving was done virtually all over, so it's impossible to say that one area specialized more than the rest, though some areas developed certain patterns, while others became better known for their ribbons and laces.

Typically, one member of the family would go out to sell these hand craft products. Which one of the family members peddled the products varied from situation to situation. Women seem to have participated since the middle of the 18th century. In 1860, fifty-four women from the village, Bonäs, went out peddling human hair products, while twenty men went out with different hand crafts. The women of Vamhus, who braided human hair into jewelry, wandered the longest distances from home. They covered an area from Glasgow to Moscow, from Lappland to Paris. It was not a large number of women that walked that far, but their example and their experiences rubbed off on others and reinforced the woman's position as independent and resourceful.

However, they spent many hours for little pay. In Gagnef, in 1912, 700 women earned a total of 12,000 Kronor at weaving ribbons (at today's rate of exchange, that would be about $3,000). Even the best ones, weaving 30 yards a day, had to work hard to make 25 cents daily.

The other form of supplementing income was arbetsvandringar "work wanderings" in which the people of Dalarna left to find temporary, seasonal work outside the province. Both men and women participated. This practice took place in other provinces, too, but on a much smaller, much more sporadic scale. For Dalarna, it became a trademark for the population, and it continues in modified form even today. The road from Stockholm to Dalarna is lined each Friday evening nowadays with cars going "home" for the weekend.

These "work wanderings" began during the 17th century. The women started to participate in the 1770's. Some were gone from Dalarna for the winter; the men chopping wood for upper class families in Stockholm, the women employed in stores and bakeries, doing textile work, etc. The largest groups were gone during the summers. The women would work at milk deliveries, rowing boats with passengers across Stockholm's many waterways, gardening, serving at coffeeshops and working at museums. . . . The list could go on and on.

People of all ages participated in the "work wanderings." During crop failures, the number was highest. During the middle of the 19th century, approximately 3500 to 4500 people in Sweden were out on "work wanderings." Ninety percent of this work force came from northern Dalarna, which at that date had a population of 70,000. From Mora, one out of every four inhabitants left; from Gagnef, one out of five. At that time, about 50 percent of the "work wanderers" were women. Of these, about 80 percent were young and unmarried. Rosander points out,

> "These 'work wanderings' were probably motivated by tradition to a much larger degree than any other type of population movement and therefore ought to be studied from an ethnological point of view. In addition to traditions, an 'inclination' toward wandering existed in Dalarna, encouraged by social pressure, a 'must.' For many, the first 'work wandering' became the sign of being an adult. It became a rite of passage."

Women became accustomed to acting independently through these trips peddling their handcrafts or working at seasonal jobs, or through taking the responsbility for running the farm while the husband was out on a "work wandering." The women became tougher in the process and soon gained the reputation for having sharp tongues and wit. This reputation stimulated the development of wit and many an anecdote still circulates describing how the kulla, as the women from Dalarna were called, always got the last word.

Northern Dalarna developed Sweden's most mobile population, as well as its most conservative peasant culture, and so it has remained into modern times. In his booklet, **Dalska arbetsvandringar före nya tidens genombrott**, Göran Rosander points out four main reasons for Dalarna's cultural conservatism, recognizing that it is difficult to say which is the cause and which is the effect.

First, the people from Dalarna had a stable historical reputation for being the saviors of the nation on several occasions. A person from Dalarna had an inner pride, a form of ethnic identity, which was nourished later when writers and painters began to explore Dalarna's folk arts. This pride also stemmed from the reputation that they were hard working and did excellent work.

Secondly, the people out doing seasonal work experienced minority problems, in part because of their ethnic identity. They proudly stuck to their local costumes, so that they could immediately be identified as **Dalmas** or **Dalkulla**. (**Mas** is a contraction of the first name, Mats, a very common name in Dalarna and pronounced '**mas**' there.) The dialects were also kept intact with pride. These factors set them apart, and that united them. Maybe in that process of opposition, a chauvinistic overemphasis on the home community's life style developed.

Thirdly, a strong social control and solidarity was maintained within the groups out on "work wanderings." A system of electing a foreman for each group had developed early. These groups can be seen as extensions of the village, where they had learned to take responsibility (each man had a vote in the village council), to obey, and report acts contrary to custom.

And last, one should note that, for the individual, the "work wanderings" didn't last a lifetime. Most participated for only a decade or so, during their late teens and early twenties. These four factors, says Rosander, interwoven into each other, help to explain the resistance of Dalarna's folk culture to change.

In addition, other aspects probably reinforced Dalarna's cultural conservatism:

    —lack of a nobility, rich landownders, or civil servants who, in other areas, brought in new ideas and innovations;
    —large villages with strong internal control;
    —no settlements outside the village that dared to break traditions;
    —a fixation on a way of life in the Middle Ages when the living standard was higher through sales of bog iron.

The women, then, working at the fäbod were proud of their heritage and reluctant to change. They were concerned with doing their best and took pride in their work. They were admired by their community, which expressed its appreciation, for example, in their homecoming rituals.

THE VALLKULLOR

Girls in the fäbod area grew up in an atmosphere of women being quietly independent, hard-working, and resourceful. Many saw their mothers earning much-appreciated extra income and their older sisters or cousins being admired as vallkullor. It was expected of the girls that they would help with the animals as well as household chores at a very early age. Anna Persson's experience in 1863 is characteristic of many a young girl's:

Cooking whey-butter outside to avoid heating the cabin.

"Before we did the buföring to the fäbod, we let the cows graze in the forest around the village. One day, I lost all my cows. To begin with, I called and searched, and finally ran home, believing they had walked home before me, but they hadn't. I had to take off my heavy wooden clogs and run out into the forest again barefoot (one can't run well in clogs). I got all the way up to our fäbod, before I found them. There they lay, all of them, in the meadow. There was nothing to do but get them up again and chase them home in the dark. It was horrible. Oh my God, how I cried, and how scared I was."

From a very early age, girls saw their mothers or their girl friends' mothers taking over complete responsibility for running the farm, coping alone with legal, economic, and personal problems, while the men were gone from home on "work wanderings", peddling handcrafts, or making and selling charcoal. The men knew that they had to depend upon their wives while they were gone, and this created early a tone of equality between the sexes. This was expressed in comments about a bride like, "She is dependable and stands on her own feet." "She is strong, healthy, and hard-working."

A girl grew up sensing the independence and self esteem of her older friends. Parents didn't arrange marriages in Dalarna for their daughters; when parents made a suggestion, the girl could say yes or no and her decision was respected. A girl also observed from very early years that women were admired and appreciated for their candor and frankness, which was often sprinkled with a quick wit.

The vallkulla was either hired for a summer or she was a family member or a maid. When a farmer and his wife needed to employ a vallkulla, certain value systems were expressed. They looked for a woman known for her dependability, her good common sense, her skills at making the different milk products, and her sense of direction in the forest. She should also be hard-working, quick, and resourceful The people wanting to employ a vallkulla often had to be out early Alfred Lindkvist explained that

".....If you wanted Gammel-Lisa, you had to be quick and ask her right after the Epiphany, or else someone else would get her. You had to wait till the day after Epiphany to ask her, for if it snowed on that day she wouldn't take the job, because she knew that snow on Epiphany meant it would be a very rainy summer."

From the young woman's point of view, it was an honor to be asked to be the vallkulla for a summer—an official recognition of her value in a society that prized hard work and responsibility and recognized the necessity of an income. The women seem to have appreciated the chance to be their own bosses and to enjoy the freedom the fäbod life offered.

The employed vallkullor were mostly unmarried and young, whereas those coming from a farmer's extended family were often much older. Quite common among the latter seems to have been a grandmother, forming a team with one or more of her granddaughters. Or it could be that a housewife took her children with her and spent the summer up in the mountains.

WORKLOAD AND SALARY

In addition to herding all day, the vallkulla was supposed to get the following jobs done: milk the cows and goats and let them out into the holding corral, strain the milk and put it aside, heat the skim milk from the day before and put in the rennet, so it would make cheese, wash all containers, clean the barn, take up the cheese and press it into a cheese mold, as well as pour the whey into the cast iron pot and put it aside. This should all be done by 7 a.m. She then spent the day herding, until 4 or 5 p.m. While she walked with her cows, she should knit stockings and socks, often one pair per family member. She should also gather branches and make specifed numbers of tools. "We were suposed to make 20 whisks, 40 small and 30 large dish- and scrub-brushes, and an endless amount of withes."

The vallkullor were also supposed to gather leaves for the animals to eat during the evening milking. Betty Andersson from Grangärde remembers,

"Almost every day, mother had to go out into the forest and strip leaves for the cows. . . . All of us three girls had to go with her. She carried my youngest sister on her arm and a special type of bag for gathering leaves hung on her back. I and my next younger sister each had a small bag on our backs, because it was just understood that we should help with the work as far as we could. I remember to this day so clearly how mother used to sing while walking among the birch saplings, ripping the leaves off one branch after the next.

"Another job which I heartily hated in those days, but which I just couldn't get out of doing, was to gather mosses from under the huge spruce trees and pull it home in a little wagon built just for that job. The mosses were used as bedding in the barn. An awful lot of moss was needed."

While the vallkulla walked, she knitted and, while she sat resting during the middle of the day, she had to sew an agreed upon number of shirts for her employer and his family.

After the vallkulla had returned to the fäbod in the afternoon, she had to milk the cows and take care of the milk, wash the dishes, keeping an eye on the wheybutter boiling (which took some seven hours). When enough cream had been collected, many a vallkulla got up an hour early to churn it into butter, because it was easier to churn in the cool of the morning.

Many times, the vallkullor formed groups and traded work. In a group of three, for instance, they rotated so that one would herd everybody's cows, while the other two shared all the work at the cabins.

It is almost impossible to say how much the vallkullor were paid, since salaries varied from area to area and from time period to time period. They received a cash payment and the food they ate at the fäbod, plus some clothing—perhaps a skirt or material for a dress or blouse, stockings, or shoes. The cash payment was never large. One woman reported that her pay per cow per summer in 1902 equalled what a man employed to help with the haying earned in a week.

Samples of cash payments

Village	Year	Per Cow	Per Goat
Transtrand	1860	2.00 kr	0
Solleron	1870	0.75 kr	0
Bjursås	1870	1.50 kr	0.50 kr
Gagnef	1880	2.50 kr	0
Djura	1890	3.00 kr	1.00 kr
Ore	1900	5.00 kr	0
Orsa	1923	15.00 kr	7.50 kr
Alvdalen	1940	30.00 kr	14.00 kr
Orsa	1950	38.00 kr	16.50 kr

* per summer; 4 kr = approximately $1 in mid-1950's

SOCIAL STRUCTURE AND VALUES

To be her own boss was one aspect of fäbod life that the vallkulla appreciated. Down in the village, she was either daughter, maid, or wife to someone and had to fit into that role, doing what she was asked to do. At the fäbod, she was in charge of her own time and she could arrange her own work and, to some extent, determine how she would do it. Vallkullor, for example, often helped each other out, so that there would be free time for visiting.

The vallkulla also appreciated the opportunity the fäbod life provided to show that she was capable of doing the job and doing it well. She took over the responsibilities for the cows and goats when she left the village, and her desire was to return them fat and healthy. The day of the return, the housewife inspected and commented upon the amount and quality of the milk products and the hand crafts. To the vallkulla, it was of utmost concern to produce as much as possible; the housewife, who in her young day had very likely worked as a hired vallkulla, knew this and complimented the girl.

The personal freedom the fäbod life provided was very much appreciated by the young unmarried vallkullor. During the winter months, there were very few opportunities to meet boys from other villages, for the young men of a village saw the girls of their home village as belonging to them and kept other boys out as much as possible. But during the summer, the boys were free to walk up and visit wherever they wanted. Since each fäbod had girls from many villages, the summers became a period of mixing and making new friends. Not only did they appreciate meeting new boys, but vallkullor of all ages were also glad for the opportunity to meet girl friends from previous summers and make new friends among the ones they met out in the forest while herding.

The vallkullor who returned to the fäbod each summer for decades deeply appreciated the close contact with nature, the beauty of the mountains, and the peace and quiet. Many sentiments like the following were expressed during interviews. "It is not summer if I don't get to go up to the fäbod." "I can't conceive the possibility of spending a summer in the village." "She liked nature more than people and really loved her summers up there." "We used the fäbod as long as grandma was living. The last few years, she took only one cow up with her. It was like a therapy, for she just needed it." Lilly Sterner-Jonsson explained:

"This longing, this psychological need to get up to the fäbod in the summer, I saw so clearly in an old woman who was too weak to walk up to the fäbod any more. She stood in the village, holding on to a tree, looking up to where her fäbod was, crying so hard."

Many women expressed an appreciation for the opportunity the fäbod life gave them to be alone with grandma. Between these two generations grew up a strong feeling of togetherness, of camaraderie and love. This is expressed over and over in their desire and the pride in "doing like grandma did."

Value systems imprinted in the village carried over to fäbod life, of course. One of these values was the strong desire for cleanliness. "We wanted it pretty and clean around us at the fäbod," I heard many a time during the summer I did this field study. One would think that living under rather primitive conditions, where water sometimes had to be carried very far, the vallkullor would have slipped into a habit of easing up on cleanliness, but they didn't. Of course, it was absolutely essential to keep all the milk containers scrubbed and clean, or else the milk products would spoil. But not only were these kept clean, the cabins and barns were too.

The women took pride in and enjoyed having their surroundings as beautiful as possible. The bed with an abundance of laces, the wildflowers brought in, the spruce branches on the floors, the birch branches around the walls, the white washing of the corner fireplace, the high polish of the copper coffee pot lid, are all expressions of these values and desires.

A vallkulla with birch-bark back pack and a cow horn for sending signals to her cattle.

A nine-year old valkulla. (Dalarna Museum.)

Making cheese at the fäbod.

This aesthetic sense, this longing to beautify one's surroundings, wasn't something a vallkulla was born with. She learned it by being a part of the group from an early age. Many a vallkulla started when she was 12-14 years of age. It took her some years of training before she was capable of maintaining the standards set by the older women, but she had their loyal support and help while learning. Anna Persson's memories are typical:

> "Lena and I were 11 and 13 years old the first time we worked as vallkullor. There was an old woman, Åhs-mor, in Perol's cabin nearby. She woke us up every morning and saw to it that we got going. She taught us a lot and she was so friendly to us."

Often, it turned out that one of the women became a leader and took on the responsibility of seeing that the group functioned and cooperated and helped the youngest ones. She settled arguments and difficulties as they arose among the vallkullor concerning questions of infringement on other's grazing, lack of cooperation, and such, as well as petty arguments of all kinds. But all was not necessarily smooth between the older and younger generations of vallkullor. Some old, bossy vallkullor were not always liked by the younger ones:

> "Old Kajsa-Lisa had been at the fäbod 40 summers and she knew everything and bossed everybody around. Everybody respected her, but this particular summer, nobody had hired her, and that was a cause for rejoicing among the younger vallkullor."

Occupational jokes about the vallkullor seem not to have existed. The reason for this is most likely that they were held in such high esteem and were admired in the villages. Since the economy depended to such a large degree on what the cows produced, the vallkulla's position was not at the lower end of the social scale. The one the group's food supply depends upon does not become the butt of a joke.

CHAPTER SEVEN

ORGANIZATION OF THE FÄBOD

The organization of the fäbod teams was a necessity. Since such a large part of the survival of the over-populated area depended on the existence of fäbodar, and since the forest grazing had become crowded, it couldn't be left to operate without tight organization and teamwork.

The villages had developed a rather strong self-government by the 18th century. Every landowner in the village was a member of the village council and had a vote in its affairs. When fäbod teams were formed, the members relied on their experiences in running the village. A fäbod team consisted of everyone who owned a part of that fäbod settlement, and all participated in its affairs. The fäbod team did not have the same members as a village team, since farmers from different villages could be owners in one fäbod.

The organization of the fäbod teams varied slightly from area to area, but basically they handled the same types of problems. The members would meet two or three times a year to discuss business. A chairman was elected for one or two years. When he called a meeting, the following questions would have to be settled:

1. The dates for the move to and from the fäbod were agreed upon. From Boda, it is reported that the farmer who owned the most cows suggested the date. Rules were established concerning these dates about 1670. In many areas, the dates seem to have been set according to weather conditions; an early spring meant an early move to the

fäbod. In other areas, particularly in the later phase of the fäbod period, the established dates often corresponded with the elementary school's summer vacation, June 6 to August 24. Practices varied almost endlessly from village to village in northern Dalarna and from one time period to the next.

Because of the scarcity of grazing, it was of vital importance that everyone moved to and from the fäbod on the same day. Arguments and hard feelings resulted when one farmer took his cows up to the fäbod earlier than the others and let his cows eat the grass that belonged to everyone. Nor could anyone stay behind when the others moved up to the fäbod and let his cows eat the grass in the area surrounding the village, since that grass was supposed to be saved for everyone to share after the homecoming in the fall. These rules eased at the turn of the century, when farmers began to grow hay in fields, but tradition often won out and everybody walked to and from the fäbod on the same day. The fäbod team would establish fines for those who broke these rules, or refer the cases to district court.

The different fäbod teams would announce their dates of moving publicly. In Leksand, it was announced in the church yard after the Sunday service was finished. In that church yard, there was a type of Hyde Park corner, where anybody could make announcements or air complaints. The chairmen of the fäbod teams would there make public their dates.

2. Another job of the fäbod team was to agree when repairs were to be done in the spring. The trail to the fäbod had to be checked and cleared of debris or fallen trees. Bridges had to be repaired as necessary, and floating log bridges over bogs had to be checked. Fences at the fäbod had to be inspected and repaired. Every member of the team had to participate in this work. Each one knew which stretch of trail or which segment of the fence was his responsibility. The job was usually divided according to the share of ownership in the fäbod or the number of cows.

3. Agreement had to be reached if slash and burning was to be done to increase the grass yield in the forest. If so, a permit had to be obtained from the district court and the work done in early spring.

4. Agreement had to be reached if **mulbetesrensning** should be done. This involved clearing fallen trees, bushes, or dead branches from the grazing area, and trimming trees to let more light to the ground.

5. As long as there was a threat from wolves and bears (up until the middle of the last century in some areas), many of the teams agreed upon dates for all-out hunts. Everybody had to participate.

6. If logging was to take place, some fäbod teams handled that matter. In other areas, this was handled by the villages, or by the

Fäbod teams repaired fences in spring.

county.

Many fäbod teams settled disputes over grazing themselves, or punished trespassers and set fines for those who neglected to participate in the team's work. Other teams brought their arguments over grazing rights and complaints about trespassing to court.

THE GRAZING TEAM

The main purpose of the grazing teams was to divide the available grazing into segments and, through a complicated system, rotate the area where each team grazed each day. The grazing routine is one example of the fäbod's adaptability to the environment.

A fäbod settlement could have as many as 20-30 cabins. Some cabins were owned by one farmer, while in other areas, a cabin could be owned by two or three. If a fäbod settlement was very small, say two or three cabins, the fäbod team and the grazing team would be one and the same, but this was rare. Most commonly, each fäbod team would be divided into several grazing teams.

A grazing team could also consist of two to four farmers who owned

One valkulla has a birch-bark rain shield.

cabins close to each other, or who jointly owned a cabin. They would employ one vallkulla to take care of their cows for the summer. Before the Redistribution, this often meant from May to September. The team met in the spring and agreed upon which woman they wanted. In reality, it was often the wives that got together and decided upon the matter and contacted the vallkulla. Many charming descriptions exist of how this was accomplished. The grazing teams agreed upon the payment the vallkulla was to receive for her work. The team also had to agree upon the work they had to perform at the fäbod: repairs of buildings, woodchopping, and cutting hay in the jointly owned meadow next to the fäbod.

CHAPTER EIGHT

AN INTERVIEW WITH LISS ANNA

To give the reader a more concrete and more personal description of a a vallkulla's life, I have included here a condensed transcript of an interview with Liss Anna, which I made in Gagnef in January, 1976. When I visited her, she was in the process of writing down her fäbod experiences for a niece, who wanted to know more about what it was like to be a vallkulla.

I was born in 1899 and I worked at our fäbod, Ösjöbuan, fifty-one summers, from 1910 to 1961. First, I took care of my parents' cows and later, when they retired, my brother's.

My very earliest memory is connected with the fäbod. I was three years old and sitting on top of a wagon one warm summer day, riding up through the forest to our fäbod. My brother, who was six years old, had to walk the last three miles, because the wagons could not go further, since the last stretch of the trail was only two feet wide.

When I was a child, grandma worked at our fäbod each summer. She sang a special song, the Ösjö-melody, when she walked ahead of the cows each morning, taking them to the forest grazing, and I sang that same song for fifty-one summers. Our cows recognized that song so well. The minute grandma started singing it, the cows began to walk towards the forest.

Grandma had so much to tell. Evenings during the winter at the farm and at the fäbod during the summer, she often sat by the fireplace, knitting and telling stories about her father who was bear- and wolf-trapper, telling tales of trolls and other forest spirits she really believed in. She also taught us what to do if we got a toothache, which plants to collect in the summer and how to use them, and what we should do to protect the cows from the trolls. She made sure we knew not to pour hot water on the ground at the corner of the fäbod, for the little underground people had their home there. Grandma told us how her mother's generation had "danced out the trolls" from the fäbod cabin on the very first day they got up there each spring, but I have forgotten what she told me. We sure never "danced out the trolls," but our summers went by without any problems anyway.

Grandma was good at telling about things. She was also well-known for her singing. She knew so many songs that disappeared with her. She remembered them herself, but would never sing any of them after she had joined a revival movement.

The summer I was eleven years old, I was alone at our fäbod, taking care of four cows, two heifers, and the goats. There were two other fäbodar in the same clearing in the forest where two older women lived, so I had neighbors to ask for help when I needed it.

When we first came to the fäbod in the beginning of the summer, we had to air out the cabin and scrub it clean, hang out the bedding, put the wooden vessels in the creek so they would swell up and become watertight, and then milk the cows. No wonder we fell asleep as soon as we were in bed. My parents stayed a few days, helping me get organized and seeing that I knew how to make butter and cheese. That summer, we had a wooden butter churn and it was very difficult for me to work it, as it splattered so badly. I cooked whey-butter in a big cast iron pot over an open fire.

My parents went home to take care of all the work on the farm, and I was left alone. Soon after, I started to get homesick. My cooking wasn't so great. I lived mostly on milk with bread soaked in it. Several times that first week, I would ask the neighbor ladies, "I wonder what they are doing at home now?" and they understood that I was pretty homesick. They both believed in trolls and such, and they knew how to cure homesickness. One day while I was outside, they carved a sliver off the unpainted table in my cabin and then they took a splinter from the threshold and put these in my coffee pot. I drank coffee every day. The next day, I felt hungry and made myself a big sandwich. The ladies just smiled at me when I told them I had eaten. After that day, I was enchanted by the fäbod and only yearned for the day I could get up there each summer.

My neighbor, Trum-mor, woke me up at 4:30 every morning. That summer, it took me two hours to do the milking. Oh, how my wrists hurt! We had to have the cows ready to be let out to graze by 7 a.m. At that time, a woman at a fäbod higher up the hill blew the "let the cows out" melody on her cow-horn, and all of us walked our cows to the grazing area selected for that day. All the women knitted while they walked, and I soon started doing that too.

A gnurka for grinding coffee.

After leaving the cows to graze in the forest, I walked back to the cabin. If it was sunny, I put my sheepskin bedding out in the sun to get warm. In the late afternoon, I would fold it over and it would still be warm when I went to bed. Then I had to clean the barn and put in new hay for the cows to eat in the evening. Most days, I made a cheese in the big cast iron pot. It held almost ten gallons of milk. A couple of days a week, I made butter, but I often got help with that job the first summer. I cooked the whey almost all day long, till it became whey-butter. In later years, people walked up to our fäbod, wanting to buy both cheese and wheybutter, but they loved it so much at home, I never did sell much of what I made. Besides, it had to last us all winter. On the farm, we stored the cheeses in a damp cellar and there the cheeses ripened just right. They tasted so good.

In July, my parents came up to cut the hay in the meadows and on the bogs. They stayed for two weeks. When they went home, they left my six year old sister, so I wasn't alone any more.

A few days after my parents left, one of my heifers had a calf, so I was alone when she had to be milked for the first time. I was so scared I cried. I walked close to her and turned away and cried some more She looked so long-legged and dangerous. I prayed to God she wouldn't kick me. Finally, I got up enough courage and sat down beside her and stroked her udder very gently and, as I did that, she stuck out her tongue and began licking me, intensely, on my arm. If they lick you, then you know they are nice. I started to milk her and she stood very still, and no kick did I get. She became our bell-cow the next summer and kept that job for seventeen years, and never ever did she kick. She was so faithful, but then she did get a lot of loving too.

The two ladies nearby really believed in Randa, "the lady of the forest," and they told me many stories about her. One family had once lost all their cows. They were gone for three weeks. They came back after the ministers in three churches had announced that they were missing. They were fine and fat, but had no milk. Everybody believed Randa had held them. In the fall, when the mushrooms started to grow, the cows were reluctant to come home. I had to walk out into the forest towards the creek each evening and call them. The women had warned me about getting too close to Storfallsbäck (Big Falls Creek), because Randa lived there. One evening, my cows didn't come home and I just had to walk out into the forest to search for them. I got close to the creek. It was gushing down the mountain side and making a dreadful noise. The forest around the creek was so dense and thick that it was dark in there, even in the middle of the day. I had to find my cows, so I walked closer and closer to the creek. I was really scared. When I got to it, it was totally dark, and I saw two glowing eyes on the other side of the creek. I was sure it was Randa! My heart almost stopped, and I turned and ran. As I did that, I let out as strong a cow-call as I could, and then I heard something absolutely wonderful: my cows bellowed and splashed across the creek. I hadn't seen their dark bodies, just the bell-cow's eyes. Their udders were full and the creek deep and cold, so they had just stayed on the other side until I came and called them. It was dark by then, but the cows knew their way home, so I just put my hand on one of them and followed. It was only that first summer that my cows didn't come home without my going out to find them.

The summer I was thirteen years old, one of my cows was bitten in the face by a poisonous snake. The cow swelled up and her head hung in an odd way. She looked awful. Trum-mor, my neighbor, told me to run to the village, Brötjärna, and ask for some medicine there. But when I got there, a man said, "Run to Mockfjärd. My brother there has something. He's just come back from the army, so he might have some medicine." But he didn't have anything. He told me to run to the Finn in Rista village. He had some ermine meat. You see, ermine are very poisonous, so they catch them and then they dry the meat and chop it up. This then becomes the antidote.

A woman came from the next-door farm and asked me if I knew how to ride a bike. When I said I could, she lent me hers, so I could ride to Rista. That was half-way home! I came to the farm and asked for the old grandpa. He came out. He was an old and very dry-wrinkled man, and I asked him if he had any ermine meat. "Maybe I have." When I told him my cow had been bitten by a snake, he gave me some dry meat and told me, "Maybe it'll help. But you should also milk the cow dry and let her drink her own milk, as the poison gets into the blood and into the milk too, and that is a good cure. Be sure to milk her dry to the last drop." He made a cone with some newspaper and put some chopped ermine meat in it, saying, "Stick this down her throat as far as you possibly can and then hold her head up high so she can't spit it out. Remember that, as it is important. Then milk her dry."

Then I had to face that long way back up to the fäbod. When I returned the bike at Mockfjärd and thanked the lady, she said, "Sit down and I'll give you some blueberry pudding." Oh, how wonderful I thought she was. I was so hungry and sweaty.

When I got back to the fäbod, the cow was lying down, looking like it was all over for her. I was frightened, but I managed to open her mouth with one hand and put the ermine meat down her throat with the other. I was really scared that she would spit it out, so I held her head up high as tight as I could and she swallowed it. Then I milked her as I had been told and gave her the milk to drink. Can you imagine, she got better almost instantly. The next morning, she was fine.

Many evenings, we used to go and sit in Britta's kitchen. Her cabin was very close to mine. She had nine children, so she would say, "Come over to me when I've gotten the little ones into bed." We spent many, many evenings there, knitting and singing and listening to Trummor's tales.

Thinking back to those summers at the fäbod, one forgets most of the troubles and worries and remembers only the funny and happy times. It was really so far to walk, so we didn't have many visitors, until a logging road was built nearby. Then a lot of friends came to visit. We used to sing a welcome song I wrote.

Välkommen hit till buan,
till den röda lilla stugan
(Welcome to our fäbod,
to the little red cabin).

I served the visitors a kind of soured milk and coffee. That coffee pot stood ready in the corner of the fireplace all day long. We sang a lot of our own songs that showed how much we loved the fäbod and how we appreciated being there.

After the logging road was built, we used to have church services at the fäbod once every summer. They baked a lot of buns and cookies and brought them up from the village. In later years, when we got a stove put in, we baked the bread ourselves.

I remember one summer when a people-hating billy goat got into the sermon. The people were sitting in the newly-cut meadow and the minister was standing in front of them with his Bible in hand. The goats had taken off with the cows to the forest early in the morning, but when they heard the hymn, they returned to the fäbod. All of the hundred or so persons sitting there knew about the people-hating goat, so the suspense rose as the goats came close to the buildings. The herd stopped at the edge of the forest and only the billy goat walked up like a king behind the minister and gave him a gentle butt on the back of his knees. The minister was a practical man, so with Bible in one hand, he reached down with the other and scratched the billy goat between the horns. This billy goat was only used to people running away from him. We don't know how long this would have lasted, but the other goats at the edge of the forest didn't like the words of God, so they ran back into the forest. When the billy goat heard this, he left his victim and ran off with the other goats.

When the big dairy was built in the middle of the 1940's, most people didn't take their cows to the fäbodar up in the mountains any longer. Only Britta and I kept it up another fifteen years, until 1961. In 1964, a car road was built, so now the peace and quiet is gone from the fäbod, but it's nice for an old lady like me to ride all the way up there now for a picnic or a fäbod church service.

CHAPTER NINE

SING THE COWS HOME!

"The work of the fäbod was done to music." I venture to say that in no other occupation has there been so much singing as in the vallkulla's work," writes Lars-Göran Stenvall. The day often started for the vallkulla with her singing or humming while milking the cows. When the cows were ready to be taken to the forest, one vallkulla, either the oldest or the one that sang or blew the signal horn the best, or the one living highest up, would sing or play the 'let the cows out' melody. The gates were opened and the cows and goats, with a singing vallkulla ahead of them, walked the cattle lanes out to the forest. In the days when the vallkullor followed the herds all day, they interacted with the cows through singing almost the whole time. The vallkulla would sing to inform the cows where she was or to signal them through song or by playing on her horn when she wanted them to come along, or start eating, or follow the group to the resting place at noontime, or to leave the area and walk home in the late afternoon. The women working at the fäbod could hear the herding vallkulla's singing, mixed with the bells, long before they could see them coming home.

A large part of the music at the fäbod was thus a work tool. Anna Johnson explains:

"Fäbod music is the oldest, most traditional, and most developed form of work music that has ever existed in Scandinavia. Its peculiar form springs directly from its function. It is intimately connected with specific work tasks and is shaped to function as effectively as possible in that context.

"Fäbod music is also one of the most interesting examples we know of communication between people and animals. . . . A well-developed system of signals existed: attention-getting calls, 'come-here' calls, as well as directional, encouraging, and scolding calls, but also soft carressing sounds of endearment and friendship. . . . Through singing-small-talk, mixed with melodious, richly ornamented herding calls, the vallkulla had constant contact with her animals throughout the day-long herding. With the help of wooden horns and cow horns, or through strong herding calls in an extremely high pitch (called kulning), they could reach the animals miles away and make them come home to the fäbod at night. But the instruments could also have the opposite function. Through howling and screaming in the wooden pipes and the coarser horns, the vallkulla managed to scare away threatening bears and wolves."

Fäbod music also filled a function in communication between people. The vallkullor used a clearly established system of signals to contact each other out in the forest, as well as to signal from one fäbod to the next, and in some cases even between fäbod and village.

Nothing connected with fäbod life is better remembered, treasured, and romanticized than its music, both vocal and instrumental. While I sat among the wildflowers at Hedåsens fäbodar one early morning in July 1980, I understood why. Five hornblowers stood in different meadows sloping down toward the fäbod buildings. They took turns blowing a fäbod melody each on cow and goat horns. These instruments have a warm and melancholy sound, a yearning tone that softly rolls over the forested hills. Once you have heard it, it stays with you—across oceans and years.

A few days later, I heard the very same hornblowers down in the village at an outdoor concert. It did not sound the same. It must be, then, that something in the acoustic resonance of the moss-covered ground and thick spruce trees, combined with the openness of the rolling hills and the lakes, gives fäbod music its characteristic quality. Several vallkullor have commented on this: "I just can't sing the herding melodies any other place than at the fäbod. It doesn't sound right in the village." "I need our mountains to sing." Thilda Blomquist explained that she had been asked to sing, standing on a mountain above timberline, during a recent trip to Lappland. "It was like singing with a bucket over my head, or against a wall. The sound didn't go any place. It just disappeared."

Another vallkulla explained to Hakan Eles that a some folklorists with their recorders came to her home in the villages and wanted her to sing fäbod melodies — "but I refused. I told them I couldn't sing in the village. I don't have the power down here."

The fäbod vocal and instrumental music can be heard for miles. "The tones rolled down the mountains," explained Thilda Blomqvist. Robert Helmer mentions some distances:

> **"Music is the medium which allows the herders to bridge the spatial gap up to a distance of about eight miles. Several of the informants confirm this. Emma Molin said calls could be heard five kilometers (three miles). Ingeborg Persson and Britta Moberg calculated a ten kilometer carrying range. Anna Nordenberg recalled that herdswomen called from the hill-tops to the villages below, and the villagers answered their calls."**

Fäbod music does trigger a romantic response. After hearing some fäbod music played up at the fäbod, I better understood the emotional and romantic descriptions of it that I came in contact with. The old people who were familiar with the music when it was still a work tool, often expressed feelings of loss. "Oh, you should have heard how the forest vibrated with music!" "I wish I could describe it to you how beautiful, how serene the fäbod songs were. I'll never forget how those tender, yet strong, melodies echoed in the forest." One old-timer explained rather romantically to Karl-Erik Forsslund that "If it was sunny and the soft wind gently hummed like light dreams accompanying the vallkulla's crystal clear, vibrating herding calls out in the forest— then it felt like I was gliding through the kingdom of heaven—yes, it was a jubilation for the soul and spirit."

There are several difficulties connected with the study of fäbod music. Its original function as a work-tool no longer exists. Only in a very few, isolated places are the herding melodies still being sung at work. Also hornblowing is no longer done by the women at the fäbod; instead it is mostly performed by men at folk music festivals, at programs sponsored by local museums or crafts guilds, or for tourists visiting fäbodar.

When the interest in collecting folk music swept over Sweden in the early 19th century, fäbod music did not get its fair share of attention. It was too far to walk for most collectors, for one thing, but, more importantly, the methods available for transcribing music were insufficient for fäbod music. Some fäbod music does not use the chromatic scale and the collectors knew no other notation. They tended to adjust 1/4 notes to 1/2 notes and ignore glides. Carl-Allan Moberg writes in his article about herding songs, "We must always remember that the notations we are studying only biasedly, obscurely, and ambiguously reflect the musical reality, about which we have slim knowledge."

Anna Johnson points out yet another problem.

"As far as I know, there exists no transcriptions made directly in the context of the different work tasks. One really can't expect that either. Not even the most skilled listener would be able to follow the animals' wanderings through the forest with pen and paper in hand and, at the same time, write down the vallkulla's song. Disconnection from the functional framework, with all that it meant of change, simplification, and even distortion, was inevitable before the days of tape recorders."

By the time the early tape recordings were being made of folk music, the very best of the fäbod music had disappeared. The recordings that were done are not the true fäbod music either. It was too far to carry the heavy equipment, so the recordings were done in the villages. These early recordings fail to reflect the true function of the music, the one intimately connected with the animals and the different work situations. Recordings done in later years by Svenskt Visarkiv (Swedish Folksong Archives) are superior from this point of view, but they were done at a time when only a fragment remains of the rich fäbod music.

MUSICAL INSTRUMENTS

There were three principal instruments used at the fäbod: a long wooden pipe call a **lur**, trumpet-like instruments made of cow or goat horns, and flutes made either of hard wood or willow bark.

THE LUR

The lur is a very long pipe, without finger holes and made of wood and often covered with bark strips. This instrument was used almost exclusively at the fäbod, where its main function until the middle of the 19th century was to scare off wolves and bears. In some areas, it was called "bear-lur," while in others it was called "wolf-lur." The instrument makes an awful noise, which scared beasts when they came close.

After the middle of the 19th century, the **lur** was no longer much in demand, since beasts were disappearing. Judging from a complaint from the 1860's, I think this must have been a relief to many: "If it rained, the wolves were particularly trying. Then the only thing one could do was blow in that lur all day long. I got all swollen and aching in my cheekbones."

Since the **lur** can be heard some eight to ten miles, its main function, after the beasts were gone, was blowing messages to other vallkullor, or down to the village if the distance wasn't too far. They used the **lur** like a megaphone, speaking or calling on it. In this manner, words were thrust into it. Not only emergency messages were sent, but also invitations to other vallkullor to come over for an evening, welcome greetings to boys when they were heard walking up on Saturday night, and so on.

A **lur** is made from two pieces of wood, which form the two halves that are to be joined together. The outsides are first shaped with a knife. Then each half is hollowed out with a curved knife. The groove had to be smooth and polished, else the instrument would be "hoarse." The groove was wider toward the lower end and thinner at the blow end. The two halves were carefully joined with pitch and held together with wooden spikes. Pitch or tar was applied to the outside to ensure tightness. Thin spruce or juniper roots or birch bark strips were then wound around the entire length of the instrument.

THE BIRCH BARK LUR

Since the **lur** was so long and cumbersome, it was usually kept at the fäbod and not brought along into the forest. If the vallkulla needed a megaphone-type instrument, she could make one with the material at hand — bark. The bark-**lur** could be made in a few minutes and discarded at the end of the day, since it wilted rather quickly. The vallkulla cut a spiral in a birch, spruce, mountain ash, or sallow tree trunk. The bark was then peeled off the tree and wound into a long cone, about a half-yard to a yard long. The wide end of the spiral was fastened with a little stick, so it wouldn't unwind. The blow hole was shaped with the fingers.

Shorter and wider bark-**lur** could be made, too, and used for blowing simple melodies. To change the tone, the hand was inserted at different angles and depths into the cone opening. Since everybody was familiar with what message each melody carried, the vallkulla could communicate with people and animals out in the forest.

HORNS FROM HORNS

Unlike the **lur**, the horn continued to be a living, functional instrument, well into this century, although today, it is used primarily as a performance instrument. When Anders Zorn arranged a folk music festival at Gesunda mountain in 1906, mostly women—vallkullor— performed on the horn. In 1980, at a week-long folk music festival at Lake Siljan, there was not one woman blowing it. In 1906, the horn was a work tool; today, it is a performance instrument.

Horns were used all over Sweden, but, during the latter part of the 19th century, the use of horns seems to have disappeared, except in isolated areas, Dalarna in particular, where they have been used at the fäbodar into our days, says Andreas Oldeberg, who has studied the 130 herding horns at Nordiska Museet in Stockholm. Most of these horns come from the fäbod area in Dalarna. One of the oldest known horns (kept at Dalarnas Museum) was used in southern Dalarna as early as the 10th century. Since it has four fingerholes, it was probably used as a musical instrument. Some of the horns were prized as instruments. The "Hedemora" horn, for example, has a base tone of

Pelle Jacobsson, showing how a horn should be played.

E-flat. If the hole farthest from the blow hole is left open, the horn produces an E and thereafter opening holes gives F, G, and A. A horn from Rättvik has a tone of F above middle C when all the holes are closed. One hole open gives F-sharp, and thereafter opening holes gives G and G-sharp. A small cow horn from Nas makes G above high C, A, B-flat, and high C. No two horns sound alike, or are in the same key, so they are therefore blown singly. A short horn has a higher pitch, while a longish, wider horn has a deeper tone.

When an animal was slaughtered, the horns were taken off and either put in boiling water or left in the dungpile for a year in order to remove the marrow. Four kinds of horns were used: the goat horn has the softest tone, the cow horn the deepest, and the billy goat and ox horn sound terrible. When the horn was clean, a blow hole was drilled in the narrow end. The number of finger holes was determined according to the size and shape of the horn. These holes were most often made for the left hand's fingers and were placed on the convex side of the horn, on the outer, widest side of the horn. Many horns were left undecorated, while others had owner's marks, years, and initials carved into them. A horn from Naas must have been especially good and appreciated, as it carries several vallkullor's initials from 1771 to 1880. It will play the tonic chord in both major and minor keys. The horn is difficult to blow. How many notes a vallkulla can play depends on her skill and the toughness of her lips. "It's extra difficult to blow the horn when one doesn't have any teeth any longer," explained one old vallkulla with smile. Pelle Jacobsson, one of the finest contemporary players, expressed both amazement and admiration for a vallkulla who is said to have blown dance music on a horn, when no other instrument was available. "I can't understand how she did it. I wear out after a few tunes."

FLUTES

There were two kinds of flutes used at the fäbod, not as work tools, but for entertainment, while herding or when the vallkullor visited each other in the evening. One is the willow pipe or whistle; the other is the **spilåpipa**, a recorder made of a harder wood.

The willow pipe could be made only in the late spring and early summer while the sap was flowing in the trees. A straight branch, ten to twenty-two inches long was cut. The bark was tapped lightly with a knife handle until loose; then it was twisted off carefully. This bark became the pipe. A plug was made and inserted in the top and a wedge-shaped hole cut below, just as with pipes all over the world. Finger holes were carved before the wood was twisted out.

Many folksongs and herding songs could be played on this pipe. It probably cheered up many a long boring day for the younger vallkullor. Richard Dybeck wrote in 1856 that

> "the willow pipe was entertainment for the vallkullor during the noon rest. The softness of the tone created a softness in the melodies that were played only on this pipe. A simple and old fashioned language speaks in these pipes."

These tunes Dybeck talks about are lost, since the willow pipe is now only a child's toy for a day.

Some researchers believe the **spilåpipa**, a simple wooden recorder, might have been used a lot more at the fäbodar than 19th century folk music scholars indicate. Almost all of the old **spilåpipor** in museums come from the fäbod area, and they are mentioned in writings only from the same area. When the use of the fäbodar declined, so did the use of the **spilåpipa**.

Anders Zorn encouraged Sväs Anders Ersson from Älvdalen, to come to the music festival at Gesunda mountain in 1906 and play the melodies he had learned as a child at the fäbod on his **spilåpipa**. At that time, Sväs Anders was virtually the only one still making and playing the **spilåpipa**. When Sväs Anders died in 1968, 96 years old, he had taught several generations of folk musicians to make **spilåpipa** and play herding songs, folk songs, polskas, and other melodies.

Today, every elementary school student in Dalarna learns to play this instrument in a program originated, sponsored, and directed by Dalarna's Museum. Thus the fäbod music continues to live, even if it is outside the fäbod atmosphere.

VOCAL MUSIC

Vocal music at the fäbod can be divided into three different types: **locklat** "herding calls," **vallvisor** "herding songs," and folksongs. The first two were used as work tools, the third as entertainment.

LOCKLAT—HERDING CALLS

The herding calls were not sung with an ordinary voice, but a change of voice, called **kulning**, so that the voice resembled an instrument in tone quality. There are an abundance of dialect expressions for this voice-change technique: **lulla, lala, lala, kula, kuja, köka, kauke, hoja.** But I prefer and will use the term "**kulning**." Jan Ling describes the technique:

"It is not singing the way we usually think of it, but a kind of falsetto call-singing, done in a very high pitch (up to the third octave above c) that requires hard-tightened throat muscles. The air is pressed thrustingly out for each phrase. The one who hasn't learned this technique as a child has small chance learning it at all."

In his article on herding songs, Carl-Allan Moberg explains that the tightening of the singer's throat muscles "gives weak vibration and thereby underdeveloped articulation with voicing of the vowels and rounding of the lips. The sound is nasal and the tone is flat without vibrato."

Thyselius describes it a bit more romantically:

"Kulning is an ancient art inherited from unknown, long-dead generations and fused through hundreds of years to a way of life at the fäbod. It is difficult to describe the herding call, the kulning. It is a strange, primitive, wordless song, with high, clear tones and simple melancholy melodies. And in it is some secret, some yearning magic."

Anna Johnson and five other researchers from the University of Uppsala and from Svenskt Visarkiv (Swedish Folksong Archives) spent some weeks at different fäbodar, in the summer of 1977, recording the vallkullor's singing while they walked their cows to the forest. Their work offers a number of new insights. For example, Ingmar Bengtsson, with assistance from the Physics Institute and the Music Department at the University of Uppsala, contructed a sound-sequence analyzer called MONA, (34) which, in his own words, describes

"certain parts of a particular series of physical sounds and thereby information about parts of a particular performer's behavior at a certain moment (or, more exactly, between two points of time), namely in the extent and respects in which these components co-condition a series of acoustic events of which a substantial part is considered 'musically' relevant."

MONA produces a strip of paper at a rate of two to twenty-two centimeters per second, on which are recorded the time, frequency, amplitude, and loudness of a sound. Relationships between these qualities can be used to describe such musical effects as tonal attack (hard or soft), duration, synchronicity, and spread of sound levels. On MONA, for example, the short glottal stop can be registered, the abrupt sound which often ends a phrase in a herding call and which is virtually impossible to transcribe with conventional musical notation. MONA also showed that this sound does not consist of raised or lowered tones on a western tone-scale, but a totally different kind of tonal resource. "We could study not only the tone's central, keynote frequency, we could also follow it passage to see if it was held 'straight,' if it was pressed upward or lowered on its way to the next sound happening."

Using MONA data, Anna Johnson analyzed the structure of the herding calls used in the different work tasks at the fäbod. She divides a typical herding call into four different components or phrases on the basis of their functions. The first one she calls the "melismatic phrase" or melodic line; it has long, drawn-out skeletal tones that are connected by more or less rich ornamentation of a syllable or a vowel, which can be used repeatedly throughout the phrase and/or be used with a different tone quality.

Another segment she calls the "attention-getting phrase." This is a comparatively short phrase, often a descending note, one syllable long, and of short duration. This phrase usually begins with a sharp, quick attack in a high pitch, which is then connected with deeper tones by a quick glide. The attention-getting phrase is used in situations where the vall kulla wants her animals to quickly pay attention to her.

A third segment is the "name phrase." In this segment, the vallkulla would call on her animals by name, most often three or four in a group, always including the name of her bell-cow. The names are sung lower down on the scale than the attention-getting phrase.

Finally, she describes a "parlando phrase," in which the vallkulla talked to her animals. This friendly small-talk often slid into half-song or recitation.

Mixed in among these phrases were the special calls intended for the goats and in rare instances the sheep, both animals difficult to handle. The vallkulla called them by imitating their sounds, quick downward glides over large intervals to the imitative sound, pr-r-r-r, or a short stubbornly repeated tja, tja, tja on the same note. There is a bit of playful teasing in these phrases.

Anna Johnson explains that

> "these different phrases or melodic core motifs are the building blocks with which the vallkullor created their herding calls. . . The musical raw materials of phrases were linked together through an improvised, functionally oriented adding system to a short or long musical event. The phrases are clearly separated by breathing pauses, or by a longish break in the song. In this manner, the vallkulla can vary her song during the entire day, continuously adjusting it to demands; she can make it maximally effective and, at the same time, musically rich."

Anna Johnson also points out that

> "different situations and events during the herding (thus different nuances in function) are reflected in the structure of the herding songs. Large parts of the day go by calmly. The animals graze or follow nicely and it is sufficient that the vallkulla only now and then let them know in what direction she is walking. She then small-talks with them or, if they are farther away from her, calls them with long, outdrawn rich phrases—draw a bow from a few skeletal tones, or decorate them with as rich ornamentation as tradition and her own musical talent can offer. The text consists of a few easily sung vowels or simple calling words, making it into a melismatic phrase. . . they display dynamic and joyful musical creativity. In these, the woman can utilize her entire musical talent and singing technique . . . . These phrases are the richest and the ones most easily separated from their functional connections. They have, therefore, become overly represented in transcripts, at recordings, and today they are the ones sung at festivals."

Cows and goats at pasture.

One can rarely find a pattern in the over-all shape. A herding call is open-ended, continuously adjusting to the situation. As long as the work demands it, the vallkulla continues her song. Even the rhythm is open and free; the calls can't be divided into established time or beats, says Anna Johnson.

"Rhythmic flexibility is self-evident in both parlando and attention-getting phrases, but also in the basic melismatic phrase. There the skeletal tones work as "rubber bands"; they can be stretched out or shortened to fit the resting places in the flow of the melody, while the short ornamentations and gliding tones are most commonly constant in length."

THEY SING:

The basic structure and techniques of the herding calls were embodied in almost endless individual styles. From the report of the 1977 recording expedition, I have selected three vallkullor to show how background, fäbod experience, and outside influences have had an impact on their singing technique, and repertoire.

Matilda Nord (born 1898) guessed she had worked as a vallkulla some fifty summers. She started as a thirteen year old, having to herd all day long, so she learned the herding calls while they were still a tool used throughout the day. She still uses them the same way, even though she now only walks the cows to the forest in the mornings. "The cows usually walk home by themselves in the afternoon," she explained, "but once in a while I call them home just for fun. If they are nearby and I call loud enough for them to hear, they come at once. They are in such a hurry and come home running."

Matilda didn't learn the calls from her mother or grandmother, since they had no fäbod, but from the vallkullor she worked with. In spite of being almost 80 years old, Matilda sings with a strong, solid voice. She has never performed at festivals; she performs only in traditional situations. There are no influences from other manners of singing present in her herding calls, nor any attempt on her part to "sing pretty" for the audience.

Kristina Nordin (born 1906) has worked as a vallkulla since she was a child. She learned to sing the herding calls from Ingrid at Sandåvallen, who, according to many, was superb. Kristina has the richest, most varied repertoire of phrases of all the vallkullor that were recorded during Anna Johnson's field trip. Her strong, straightforward way of singing gives a remarkably old-fashioned impression, at the same time as it is highly effective.

Gölin Morlind (born 1919) started to help out with the work at the fäbod as a very young child. At age 17, she was taking care of eight cows alone, but a couple of years later she had seventeen cows. "Then

I knew I existed!" Today, she takes care of eight cows, some heifers, and one goat. The animals take care of themselves during the days, but the tourists don't. "Some days, I take care of bus loads of them, so nowadays I sing more for tourists than cows."

Gölin learned the herding calls from her mother, and she has sung them on stage, as well as at the fäbod. During the winter, she sings in a chorus in the community, so her way of singing the herding calls shows strong outside influence. Her singing has become more a museum item than a tool at work with the animals. Her herding calls are sung in long, ornamented sequences of notes, rather than the traditional, shorter calls. It's more like a song than the others', consisting of longer, continuous melody lines with no name phrases. Sometimes she uses a word, but most often only long outstretched vowels, which gives the call an almost instrumental tone value.

AESTHETIC ASPECTS OF HERDING CALLS

Those vallkullor who were recorded in 1977 are, of course, not the only ones singing the herding calls. A vallkulla in Transtrand explained, "There is no one today that follows the herd all day long, but if it is a truly beautiful day, we do it. Then we yearn for the forest and we strike up these trilling herding calls."

The use of work tools to express an artistic urge has been mentioned in the chapter on wooden tools and utensils. Anna Johnson points out that

"a close connection between the functional and the aesthetic is often expressed in fäbod culture. The tools are simple and functional, but, at the same time, express a strong desire for beauty, a yearning for ornamentation. Into the cheese molds intricate designs were carved, which identified and also beautified the cheeses; wooden spoons and butter dishes often got a little design carved into them; the whitewashed fireplace was decorated with fresh green branches; the barns smelled of chopped juniper. And the herding calls, the herding tool, was decorated with ripples, intricate ornamentations to the delight of the singer and those who heard her."

Psychological aspects of fäbod life, of course, were reflected also in the singing. The song expressed the singer's mood, whether it was homesickness, sadness, anxiety, happiness, hope. As one vallkulla said, "Mother sang according to her mood. If she was happy, we heard that in her singing."

"There are dark sides to fäbod life," a man at Klovsjö, Jämtlands province, told Anna Johnson:

"The herding calls of the early summer were light and airy. The cows came home easily without any trouble then. But in the fall, when the cows strayed in the forest searching for mushrooms, then the kulning reflected agony and anxiety. The calls out there in the wilderness were like knives. The vallkullor gave the calls all they had. Today, there is no reality behind the kulning."

OTHER USES OF MUSIC

The vallkulla used music to communicate with animals and with other people, as well as to entertain herself and others. When music was used as a communication tool, it could be sung or played on the lur and horn intermittently. Herding melodies, when sung, did not need a text to be understood by people or cattle. The melody carried the message. It is very natural, then, that voice and instruments were interchangeable to a certain extent. Many dialects have a single word which may mean either singing the herding songs or blowing them on the horn. Also, many reports of how the vallkullor treated their instruments indicate that the difference between vocal and instrumental performance was less evident than it appears to us today.

Many people still talk of how the forest reverberated in the old days with herding melodies. Each vallkulla had a horn hanging from her hip. Sometimes, she would sing her herding calls; sometimes, she would blow them on the horn. "After blowing three or four melodies, one's lips are very tired and it gets increasingly difficult to blow," said Pelle Jacobson, "so the women sang in between blowing them."

The horns, like the herding calls, were used all day long for communication with the animals. Olambritt Anna explained: "We blew the horn when the cows were to leave for the forest in the morning, when they could come to noon rest, when they should start walking home, and sometimes even just before we started the milking." When a message or call had to travel especially long distances, the voice was not sufficient, so the horn was necessary.

As a work tool, the music was communication between the women and the cows, who recognized their vallkulla and her singing, and they did answer her by bellowing. It was two-way communication out in the forest. "If a cow was missing, one could climb up on the roof of the barn with the horn and blow. The cows could hear the horn for long distances, where kulning could not reach," explained one woman. Anna Johnson told of an old lady who had been a vallkulla in her younger years. The lady listened to a tape recording of some herding calls, then said, "The cows didn't answer, so that wasn't real."

Fäbod music was also used in person to person communication. The horns were used often for blowing messages. If a cow were lost during the day, a vallkulla would climb a knoll and blow her message.

the "my cow is lost" melody, to the east and wait for an answer. If they answered with the "we have not seen her" melody, she would repeat the procedure in the other directions. If a cow belonging to someone else came and joined a vallkulla's herd, she blew the "search no more, your cow is here" melody. Everyone knew these melodies, and there were also melodies for "my cow is stuck in the bog," "a wolf or bear is nearby," "I'm sick," "my cow is sick," and so on. There were also happy messages, invitations to a cup of coffee, "come over to my noon resting place," or "come to an evening by the fireplace." When the boys were walking up to the fäbod on Saturday nights, they often played an instrument or sang, so they would be heard long before they were seen. The vallkulla could then blow the "welcome" melody on her horn.

In the evening, when the work was done, the vallkullor often blew or sang a greeting to the other fäbodar out in the forest. This greeting was called "Evening Peace" and was answered with the same melody. If there was some problem or the vallkullor were not finished working at the other fäbod, they would not answer. Many an evening, they sang or blew several different melodies of the folksong or herding song type, just for the pleasure of it and for the fun of reaching others and hearing their melodies as answers.

But the primary use of the herding melodies was as a functional work tool. Knis Karl tells of Knis Anna Jonesdotter, who was vallkulla at Mobergs fäbodar and was teaching her ten year old daughter, Brita, to play.

> "Brita was standing one evening out in the meadow behind the fäbod and practicing her horn playing. She played 'search no more, I've found your cow.' That night a farmer in the village Kilen missed a cow. He walked up the long steep trail to Moberg's fäbod, led by the melody. When he got up there to fetch his lost cow, he was told they didn't have it. Brita had only been practicing that melody. When the farmer was told that, he burst out with strong language, advising her to practice something else."

Some vallkullor became known for their skill at singing these herding calls with the **kulning** technique. They built up a repertoire that was considered their property, and it is reported that nobody really attempted to copy them. Gösta Ullberg explained that

> "often each girl had her own melodies, by which she was recognized by the the others. When the work was finished in the evenings, the vallkullor could go out in the meadows next to the fäbod cabins and sing kulning to each other at fäbodar not too far away. When, as an answer, a melody came from another fäbod, we could hear immediately who it was that returned the greeting."

There must have been unmusical vallkullor, too—women who couldn't carry a tune or even learn one. I wanted to find out how they solved that problem, and I heard comments like, "She sang more enthusiastically than well," and "She didn't have much of a singing voice, but she laid it on anyway." Anna Johnson answered the question with, "I think I dare say that every vallkulla sang. Of course, not every one sang well, but sing they had to, in one fashion or another; it was just part of the fäbod life."

MAGICAL POWERS

Since most vallkullor had spent almost every summer since childhood at the fäbod, they had grown up with the herding calls. They learned to sing them by imitation, but not copying. Since the herding calls sung with the **kulning** technique were never alike twice in a row but constantly changing according to the situation, they invited the vallkulla to be creative. Several legends tell that women who could sing **kulning** with extraordinary beauty had learned their art from Randa, the lady of the forest, who could sing better than any vallkulla. This theme is related to the belief that exceptionally good fiddlers had been taught by the water spirit, Näcken. Herding songs and folksongs, on the other hand, were learned in the same manner as folksongs have always been transmitted—by copying.

Many a vallkulla in the old days believed in the magical power of her instruments. Such instruments were also used in protective rites, to be discussed in more detail in later. About the vallkulla's song and her instruments, Jan Ling comments:

> "It was believed (they) held magical powers which could conquer not only the wild beasts, but also vittror, giants, or trolls, who were considered to be all over the forests. . . . The lur lost its magical power if it was used for playing melodies."

The vallkullor believed in the power of the lur to rid the area of beasts. At the same time, they were aware of the belief that other instruments had opposite effects. An old rhyme expresses an anxiety about having to use contradictory instruments. The rhyme, seen from the beast's point of view, was known in many variations throughout the fäbod area.

Smala videpipor och geta horn
  lyster mina öron att höra
men grova alderlurar och bocka horn
  få r mina fötter att blöda
    Thin willow pipes and goat horns
    my ears like to hear,
    but heavy alder lur and billy goat horns
    make my feet bleed.

Blisterpipor och fingerhorn
  Låta mig väl uti öra
Tjutlurar och tjuthorn
  köra mig långt bort i myra
      Wooden pipes and horns with fingerholes
      sound good to my ears.
      Roaring lur and roaring horns
      drive me way off into the bog.

A bockerhorn å alderlur
  Dä vell jä inte höre.
Men selgepipe å bjällelat
  Dä klinger i mett öre.
      Billy goat horn and alder lur
      Those I don't want to hear.
      But willow pipe and herding song
      Those ring beautifully in my ear.

Before 1850, one of the main functions of the horn, like that of the lur, was to scare off beasts. Since the horn was easier to carry than the lur, it was used more often out in the forest. The same horn used for melodies could also be used for scaring animals. Then the vallkullor said they "screamed" on the horn, trying to make it as offensive as possible. More commonly, special horns were used—ox and billy goat horns. These had no fingerholes and were often called "screaming horns." There is magic involved with these horns, too, since they were believed to have special powers. A horn that had been broken off in a fight was thought to be best and most powerful, says Richard Dybeck, but it may never touch the ground, for if it does, it loses its power.

If a horn had been blown under a birch bark roof, it also lost its power and bears would no longer be afraid of it, is reported from Venjan. "The reason for this," says Moberg, "can be no other than that the horn loses it magical power if it has been been profaned to a musical instrument and used against its nature indoors."

Horns could be invested with magic powers after they were made. From Brunsberg, it is reported that Sjur-Berit was advised to tie her horn under her dress when she got married. She did that and the horn, having been inside the church, absorbed the word of God. The hymns Sjur-Berit played on that horn scared off the beasts from the fäbod area. Sjur-Berit believed in this power of her horn, since she never had any problems from bears or wolves.

Such belief in the magical powers of horns is old. In his book published in 1555, Olaus Magnus drew a picture of a man blowing a horn during a thunderstorm. The thunder was believed to be caused by evil spirits, and one could protect oneself from lightning by blowing on a horn.

VALLVISOR—HERDING SONGS

Music was a large part of the vallkullor's entertainment. Herding songs, folk songs, religious melodies, love ballads, and even favorite school songs were sung and appreciated. **Vallvisor**, "herding songs", were among the most popular. They were used both as a working tool and for entertainment.

The herding songs differ from the almost wordless herding calls, in that they consist of a set melody and set words, like a folk song. In a way they are a sub-group within the folk song category, separated by their subject matter and usage.

The herding songs describe fäbod life, the vallkullor's experiences and emotions. "Tulleritova, twelve men in the forest," for example, describes how a vallkulla, alone at the fäbod, is attacked by twelve outlaws. They kill her cows and threaten her. She manages to get away and blow the emergency signal on her horn. People come up from the village and kill the outlaws.

Other herding songs describe life at the fäbod, such as the following:

> Jag går i vall
> > hela dagen all
> > här pa den höga åsen.
> Dagen ar lång
> > magen ar sväng
> > lite la mor i påsen
> > > Here I go herding
> > > all day long
> > > up on the high ridge.
> > The day is long
> > > the tummy is empty
> > > little did mother put in the bag.

Like the herding calls, many of the herding songs could carry messages. It wasn't the words, but the melody that carried the message. The "Tulleritova, twelve men in the forest" is an interesting example. The melody was used as an emergency call as long as there was a threat from bears. A bear was believed to be as strong as twelve men, and to avoid evoking the bear's fury, his name was not used, but he was called "Twelve man." The melody continued to be used as an emergency signal, long after the threat of bears had disappeared. The "Twelve man," the bear, became twelve men, the outlaws.

FOLKSONGS AS ENTERTAINMENT

To entertain themselves throughout the day, the vallkullor sang songs or played the willow pipe or **spilåpipa**. Most of these folk songs were in a minor key. The general consciousness in Sweden has linked the minor key of most Swedish folk music with the at times, harsh

threatening, nature of the Nordic landscape, or with the sadly mild types of landscape and the sparse populations's loneliness and sadness, or longing for a more generous landscape. After a revival movement in the valleys, many of the older vallkullor sang religious songs, the repertoire increasing with each revival. Many of the young vallkullor liked to sing tragic love ballads or love songs. Anna Bäckström, who had both grandmothers at the same fäbod settlement, commented about the difference between the two, even if they were of the same generation. "My father's mother sang a lot of love songs, but my other grandmother could never ever even think about letting anything so ungodly come across her lips."

In spite of their heavy work load, the vallkullor would get together some evenings, particularly Saturday and Sunday evenings, at one cabin, light a fire, and sing songs and tell stories while they knitted. They seem to have engaged in community singing only rarely. Common instead was the tradition of taking turns singing. Women with good voices and a good store of songs were really appreciated. Many seem to have taken well-known melodies and composed new words to them, describing their fäbod life, their desires, homesickness, or funny events. Liss Anna has a book in which she has written down all the songs she wrote new words to, and that book is almost filled.

Community singing was done when visitors were present, often in connection with dance games, which will be described in a later chapter.

All forms of fäbod music were treasured and appreciated in the old days, according to reports. This rhapsody comes from Grangärde: "She sang so beautifully that the men leaned on their scythes and the women on their rakes to listen. They couldn't work, so touched were they by the beauty of her trilling melody."

Most of the fäbod music is gone by now and is only a fond memory. Sven Floren expresses what so many feel, when he remembers his first morning at a fäbod when he was ten years old:

> "No memory from my childhood stands out with such clarity and purity, no memory is so connected with an intense feeling of happiness as that first morning. The cattle lane was just outside our cabin. I stood by the window, looking and listening. Bellowing cows and eagerly jumping goats. The vallkullors' calls, but above all else their song. With clean and clear voices, they sang these old herding melodies. Clear sky, dew-wet grass. From that moment, I was enchanted."

Many share with him this enchantment for the fäbod music that was such an integral part of fäbod life.

CHAPTER TEN

COW BELLS—THE MUSIC OF THE COWS

The tradition of bells on the animals is closely connected with fäbod life. These bells served several functions: they kept the herd together; they informed the vallkulla of the whereabouts of her animals, who could be identified through tone quality of the bells; they assisted in the search for lost animals; they informed the vallkulla if the animals were frightened by wolves or bears; and they protected the animals through magic.

Each farm had one specific, large bell, which was used only at the fäbod. It was made with more care than any of the others. This fäbod-bell stayed in the family through generations, and its tone became "the melody" of that farm, its signature. This bell was not hung on just any cow, but on a selected lead-cow, or bell-cow. To be chosen for this position, a cow must be sensible, dependable, familiar with the forest surrounding the fäbod and she must definitely be a leader.

Many a story describes how a cow reacted with pride and dignity at being selected bell-cow for the summer and how the other cows soon accepted their subordinate position. If a bell-cow misbehaved or neglected her duty, she could be punished by losing the bell to another cow. The former bell-cow would react to that with anger or sulkiness. Often, it required only one day of punishment to bring her back to good behavior, and the bell would be hers again.

In some places, all the cows from neighboring farms were let out into one meadow to get used to each other before being moved to the fäbod. In Norway, Mrs. Fönhus noticed one year that her bell-cow was acting strangely, standing behind a tree and not joining the other cows. She had about decided the cow was sick, when she noticed she had forgotten to tie on her cow bell. She sent her daughter, Ragnhild, for the bell and tied it on. Then the cow came right out of hiding, swishing her tail and swinging her hips as she proudly joined the other cows.

It was important to train the cows and goats to follow the sound of the lead-cow's bell. This eliminated the danger of one of them wandering off and getting lost. It also helped in getting all the animals home together in the afternoon during the late fäbod period, when herding all day no longer was done.

By the tone of the bell, every vallkulla at a fäbod settlement could identify the farm to whom each bell-cow belonged. Even most people in the villages knew their own and their neighors' bells by sound. When the women returned to the villages in the fall, the people could tell by the sound who was coming home, long before they could see anybody.

When I was sitting in the kitchen of the three sisters Blomqvist in Moje, Kerstin asked Anna to go out to the barn to fetch the fäbod bell, so I could see and hear it. Kerstin explained that they had two bells that looked very much alike. The bell-cow had lost her bell one summer and they had had to buy a new one, which looked like the old one but didn't sound quite the same. Two summers later, they had found the old bell and started to use it again. Now, both hung in the barn. When Anna came to the front steps, she let the bell ring just once; immediately Kerstin called out, "That's the wrong bell." So Anna had to go and fetch the right one, the older bell.

Great emphasis was placed on the tone quality of the bell: its sound had to carry over long distances, so that the vallkullor could locate the animals. "How wonderful it was to hear the sound of the bell those dark evenings in the fall when we had to hike up and down over the hills searching for our cows."

Another function of the bell was to inform the vallkulla if the animals were frightened, especially back in the times when wolves and bears were a threat. Knis Karl tells of an event where the toll of the bell conveyed the message that something was wrong: "The bell tolled and rang 'keeping time,' so they understood something was wrong. . . . . A bear had whacked the bell-cow and broke her back. She lay on her side, banging the bell from one side to the other, and that made the bell 'keep time.'"

The ritual function of the fäbod cow-bell goes back into pre-historic times. Lithberg, who has researched the history of the cow-bell, writes that "from magical concepts still connected with the cow-bell in Scandinavia, one can understand that they have had a long existence, going back into pre-Christian times. These concepts might even come from a period of primitive religious beliefs, which lie far beyond the time of the first archeological finds."

One ritual using the fäbod bell took place on the first day the cows were let out of the barn after the long harsh winter. Local practices varied, but the basic pattern was that one, two, or a combination of the following items were stuffed into the bell and given to each cow to eat as she stepped out of the barn: salt, flour, bread, hay, chaff, hair from the bell-cow's tail, and scrapings from the fäbod bell. As the cows were given this bit to eat, the following words were said, "**Har får du en tapp ur skälla, sa du går hem till kvälla.**"(Here you get a bit from the bell, so go each evening to where you dwell.)

The following ritual is recorded from the area adjoining Dalarna to the north:

"On the way up to the fäbod, the vallkulla must not forget to pick a birch branch that grew on a stump. This branch she must twist counter-clockwise and make into a circle. After arriving at the fäbod, she must fill the bell with sletje (salt and flour) and place it on the floor. Holding the birch circle with her left hand, she reaches through it with her right hand to pick up a bit of the sletje, which she offers to each cow as she enters the fäbod barn for the first time that summer. Thereafter, she sleeps with the cow-bell under her pillow for three nights. All this is done to insure that the cows will return to the fäbod each evening."

Sleeping with the cow-bell under the pillow is a local practice, much like the girls' custom of sleeping with objects under their pillows to make wishes come true.

The question of the magical power of the bell to protect the cows from evil spirits, trolls, or vittra-people has not been researched sufficiently. I found only vague statements like, "The magical and protective powers in the oldest, the wooden bell's tone, was transferred to the metal bells."

OTHER BELLS

The lead cow was given the farm's biggest and most important bell. In addition, a whole series of bells served different functions. Mischievous cows and heifers had to wear bells until they learned to follow the lead cow. Pregnant cows carried bells, and so did sick cows. Every goat was given a small bell with a rather high tone to wear at the fäbod.

The oldest metal bells were made of bog iron by the farmer himself or the local blacksmith. Later, bells were often made and sold by wandering blacksmiths who, through the generations, had developed "secret recipes" for making them. It became a trade skill handed down from father to son. One legend tells of how a smith heard an exceptionally beautiful bell on a cow in Norway. He sneaked over to the cow, took the bell off, and studied its construction, thus stealing the secret before hanging it back on the cow.

The tone quality was important, not the appearance. Each bell had to have a different tone and be able to carry that tone over vast distances. To achieve as beautiful a sound as possible in the lead-cow's bell, the housewife often donated a silver spoon or two, since silver was believed to create a prettier tone than copper or brass.

Iron was used for the core of the bell. A used ploughshare was considered best, since it was made of the hardest iron, which gave the best and loudest tone. The iron was hammered into a sheet, then cut and folded. Next, it was riveted and the sides aligned. The tongue and the strap were attached by inserting them and folding the ends of the "ears" of the bell.

Next, the bell was coated on the inside with a certain mixture of copper or brass. The smith often kept the amount a secret. Some added a silver spoon or two. Then, the bell was filled with charcoal and entirely encased in clay. This clump was put in a fire for about an hour, being turned serveral times to insure that the solder mixture inside was evenly distributed. The clump had to be slowly cooled down by being rolled on the floor. Finally, it was put in a bucket of water for about 15 minutes and the clay knocked off. The tongue was attached with pliers and the bell was ready for use.

Not just anybody could tie the big fäbod bell on the lead cow. It was the mistress of the house who performed this act. "She blessed the bell, took from the sunrays and gave to the cows, and wished them well."

The Swedes have had and still have an almost romantic longing for summer. For the farm communities in the fäbod area, the bells announced that this fantastic period had arrived at last. The bells were thus closely connected with emotion. Among the Swedes' very technical and unemotional writings about the fäbod, one can find an abundance of romantic desriptions of how the bell-tone in minor key vibrated through the forest — descriptions of beauty of a summer morning when the cows wandered off to the forest expressing harmony between the bells and the sounds of the summer forest.

One farmer, immigrating to the United States, took his fäbod bell with him. It was his most-valued possession.

CHAPTER ELEVEN

FOLK MEDICINE

In the days before modern medicine, the housewife usually treated her family and her cattle when they were ill. If the illness persisted in spite of her cures, she could get help from local healers, who, in Dalarna, were called **klok gumma** or **klok gubbe** "wise or knowledgable woman or man." Because of the distances, the women at the fäbod had to rely on themselves to a much larger degree than the women staying in the village. A vallkulla had to know how to immediately stop the flow of blood from a cut, to treat sprained or even broken bones, to treat snake bites, to treat an assortment of aches and pains, to assist at birth or calving, to be able to cure her cows' stomach upsets or diarrhea, since these ailments severely lowered milk production.

The vallkullor brought with them up to the fäbod a wide variety of the medical concepts of the time and focused them on the immediate needs at the fäbod—the care of her cows and the other vallkullor during emergencies. Since the cows were an economic asset, it is not surprising that they were treated with as much care and concern as people. In fact, many of the vallkullor's remedies were used interchangably for cows or people as the need arose, and, at times, the cows were cared for better than people. Of course, the season was to the vallkullor's advantage, for the vallkullor had relatively little call to treat influenza, ear and throat infections, etc., which were more common during the dark winter when people lived mostly indoors under rather crowded conditions.

Folk medicine can be divided into two branches—natural, herbal medicine; and magico-religious medicine. The most serious problems in both categories, especially the magico-religious, are usually left to local healers rather than individual members of a community. But such help was usually not available to the vallkulla. She had to make do with what she had. The practice of natural, herbal medicine was probably the more prevalent in the vallkullor's jobs, but they also practiced a wide variety of protective rituals, charms, and magico-transfers of minor ailments.

CONCEPTS OF ILLNESS

When a person or an animal got sick, the people often believed that external forces caused the illness. In Gagnef, they said that one had been hit by evil (**släjs ont**), which often happened near water. If a person were badly frightened, he or she could get sick, or develop a sore that was slow to heal. Illness could also be caused by another person: animals could be made sick and unable to move by Finns cursing them (**Finnskjuten**). People and animals could be made ill by **hugsning**, "staring" at the person or animal and thinking strongly about him or her. **Hugsning** can even be done unintentionally—by just strongly admiring someone.

Illness could also be caused by sickness demons, who not only cause the sickness, but *are* the sickness, too. The presence of the illness and the presence of the demon are synonymous in the people's minds. People did not seem to have a very clear conception of these demons; they just believed that they existed. Only two were personified: the cholera and the bubonic plague were seen as a young man and woman. If they were seen raking in front of a house, one person would die; if they were seen sweeping, everybody would die.

One could also get sick by breaking a taboo; touching a crow's or magpie's nest; lifting a dead snake; harming a frog. These animals derived their power from demons; so by touching them or their belongings, one touched the demons. One would get sick if one described a demon, for one thereby invited the demon to revenge and the demon would enter one's body. If one walked across a bridge without spitting, the evil spirit living under the bridge would enter one's body and cause aches in the joints. If one took a bath in a lake or river without spitting or making a stick, spitting on it, and throwing it into the water while chanting: "Take this and let me be," the water spirit (Näcken) would make one sick. By walking on the wrong side of the road, one would bump into the invisible spirits and get sudden stomach pains.

Carl-Herman Tillhagen lists several reasons for illness in his book **Folklig läkekonst**: evil persons, evil eyes, magic, spiders, lice, mice, supernatural spirits, and sickness demons. Supernatural spirits caused sickness by blowing on somebody; the water spirit (Näcken) bit; the mara sucked or rode on someone; the gnome boxed a person on the ear; the vittra-people bit, and the ghosts hugged.

Well into the 19th century, the need to explain the reasons for sickness seems to have been overpowering, judging from the almost endless reasons given for why someone got sick. The people seem to have been totally surrounded by taboos and threats. Their folk medicine therefore was a desperate attempt to ward off disease through protective rituals and to cure the victim once he was ill. These rituals and cures fall broadly into some five categories: "casting out," transfers, balms, potions, and charms, this last one often incorporating one or more of the others and usually incorporating the Christian Trinity.

NATURAL, OR HERBAL, MEDICINE

To this branch of folk medicine belongs a variety of "home remedies" which to a large extent used herbal plants. Very seldom were these plants grown at the fäbod; rather they were gathered in the forest. Most vallkullor were familiar with a variety of plants, leaves, berries, roots, and bark and would use them according to personal knowledge and preference, depending on the situation.

BALMS. Herbs and plants were often used as balms for many different ailments of people and animals alike. The women gathered and dried these plants and berries during the summer and saved them for the winter.

Pale and skinny women washed their faces in Daphne-berry tea, for example, to get a ruddy, rounder look. Daphne (**daphne mezereum**) has poisonous berries that contain mezerein, a syreanhydrid which, even in very small quantities, causes damage to skin and mucuous membrane. Washing the face in water in which some of these berries had been soaking gave the skin a blush and swelling from the irritation.

Daphne bark, dried or fresh, was used as an absorbing medication for eye infections, difficult or heavy breathing, coughing, and snake bites. The bark was applied to the affected area and changed daily for a week. Daphne was also used as a magically protective agent, and as such will be discussed in the chapter on folk beliefs.

Valeriana root (**valeriana officinalis**) was gathered before the leaves started to grow in the spring, dried, and kept in a sealed container. The smell is extremely offensive—like concentrated foot-sweat. This root was used for curing nervous disorders, cramps, and hysteria, though perhaps it was more often used for its magically protective powers than for medical purposes.

Leaves of "White man's foot" (**plantago major**) were used on corns and cracks on the feet. Lilly Sterner-Jonsson told of an odd-looking plant she had seen at several abandoned fäbodar. It had huge leaves, resembling a parsnip's. Through much research, she learned that it was a medicinal herb, **Mäster** root, which had been brought into Sweden from Switzerland by the monks. This plant was used for all kinds of sicknesses, from runny nose to childlessness. The plant was thought to be strongly aphrodisiac, so it was grown in a hidden spot at the fäbod.

POTIONS. Concoctions of herbs meant to be taken internally were, of course, very common. Potions made of herbs were used for the cows as well as for people, often in the same manner. Diarrhea in cows is difficult to cure. They gave less milk and, no matter how hard-working and responsible the vallkulla, it really was bad luck for her if the cows got diarrhea. She could feed them a "tea" made of St. John's wort (**hypericam maculatum**), mixed in with their fodder, or a combinations of several other plants.

Daphne berries were crushed and mixed with the fodder or boiled and the liquid given the cows to cure constipation or shivers. Other mixtures, for example, St. John's wort, cloves, mustard, and bread spices were boiled and given to the cows several times a day until they got well.

Color association mixed with herbal medicine in treating a sickness in cows called the "red soot." The red root of the Fivefinger (**potentilla erecta**) was cooked in water until it became a thick, red sauce, which was given the sick cow. In other areas, the same illness was treated with vitriol, but only in small amounts, for otherwise the cow would get even sicker than she was.

Flax seeds were used against constipation, sour stomach, and children's cough. Mallow (**malva neglecta**) was used as a tea against stomach disorders and as a salve on wounds. Gypsy weed (**veronica officinalis**) was brewed to a tea and drunk to cure urine stoppage. Bright's disease was treated with a tea made of juniper berries and a gentian (**menyanthes trifoliata**). Sweet false chamomille (**matricaria chamomilla**) was taken to lower fever and ward off infection.

In chapter nine, Liss Anna told how she was cured of homesickness when the other vallkullor gave her "homesickness coffee." Even cows could suffer from homesickness, writes Gagner.

"This can happen when a new cow is taken up for the first time. To cure this, they are given 'homesickness buns'. . . prepared from particular plants picked Midsummer Night, dried and cut into small pieces. Only married women can make these buns, and there are only one or two in each county that knows how—and they do not tell others the secret ingredients. These buns are sold to the ones needing them."

When a cow lost her appetite and thus produced less milk, a mixture of herbs (which ones varied locally) were given and a charm such as the following was recited: "I do to the poor animal, whichever color

it has, I send the one stealing the cow's power to the north, west, south, and east, up and down, driving the evil Satan out, not in. In the name of the Father, the Son, and the Holy Ghost."

In other areas, a cow's appetite was restored by giving her a mixture of bay leaves, gentiana roots,, and salt. In Gagnef, a woman once took a feeding bucket away too quickly from a cow, relates Gagner, "and the cow lost its courage" and started to shake like an aspen leaf. The woman took three pinches of hairs from the cow's belly, cut her ears and caught three drops of blood, and put all this on a piece of bread, which she gave the cow, who got well at once." This is a curious mixture of "casting out," transfer, potion, and charm.

MAGICO-RELIGIOUS HEALING

In Dalarna, as well as elsewhere in the world, there existed a folk belief that some supernatural powers could be tapped for healing. Since some sickness was believed to be caused by demons who sent evil forces into a person or animal, it was believed that these forces could be removed by a "counter spell," often in the form of a ritual act and/or a charm involving holy words. The vallkullor, each according to her personal experience, knowledge, and preferences, used several rituals and charms to protect or cure herself and her cows.

"CASTING OUT." One of the more common methods for treating a person or animal was the "casting out" act. This could be done by the sick person or a friend who gathered into a bundle different objects such as three straws of hair, three nail clippings, three pinches of salt, three pinches of flour, or three pinches of ashes. These ingredients were tied into a cloth. At midnight, the person would walk to a river or creek, stand with his or her back to the water and, with the right hand, throw the bag over the left shoulder into the water, saying "**Tvi, ta de dae å lått bli mä!**" (Ick, take this with ye and let be me! — sometimes the name of the sick person was included). That done, the person had to walk home silently without looking back. To really insure success, she should "touch fire" when she got home. This would be done by touching a flame or by striking a match and holding it inside cupped hands.

A variation of this cure was performed by a friend of the sick person who would make a bundle of copper, pewter, and brass pieces, and scrapings off three keys. At midnight, she set the bundle afire and walked with it three times counterclockwise around the house where the sick person was. After that, she carried the bundle to a cross-roads, put it down in the middle, and let it burn up.

Gagner reports that an old man explained that there are two kinds of "casting out." One is for the more dangerous sicknesses, when nine kinds of ingredients were needed: scrapings off iron, copper, brass, silver, and gold; pieces of the sick person's clothing, hair, nails and soot. For less serious illnesses, three ingredients were needed: a pinch of flour, three grains of salt, and fire.

Gagner feels that these different things that are thrown out should be seen as an offering to the irritated spirit to pacify him, a pawn through which the sick person gets free, so he can get well. The words that accompany the act, "take this and let me be," also indicate that the bundle is an exchange for freedom from the illness.

TRANSFERS. Illness could also be transfered to an object and the object properly disposed of. For example, if a vallkulla got a toothache, she could take a stick or a nail and touch the tooth and surrounding gums with it until the gums started to bleed. Then she would take the stick and pound it into a tree. The toothache would thus be taken from the person and given to the tree. Some trees that grew in some odd shape became *the* transfer tree and had a lot of sticks and nails pounded into them. Some of these can still be seen today.

In Gagnef, a transfer cure is reported for "the creakies," an inflamma- tion of the wrist. Only a first-born child could cure this ailment. The creaking wrist was placed on a chopping block; the child holds an axe with both hands and chops into the block on one side of the wrist while the sick person asks, "What are you chopping into?" The child answers, "I'm chopping the creakies from the wrist into the wood of the chopping block." Then the child repeats the ritual on the other side of the wrist, and finally repeats it once more on the first side. Thus the child chops three times and the question-answer ritual is repeated three times.

Anna Bäckström had a sty in her eye one summer at the fäbod in the 30's. An old vallkulla told her how to "cut it out." She should strad- dle the threshold of the cabin and touch the sty with a stick three times, saying "I cut this sty from the eye." Anna followed the advice, but the sty stayed on.

The number of acts to remove warts is virtually endless. Most com- mon seems to be to transfer the wart to a tree, stone, crossroads, or river. The wart was often touched by an object that was to be disposed of—splints, coins, red yarn, etc. Warts could be "counted away" or "tied away" by making as many knots on a string as one had warts and then burying the string. When it rotted, the warts would be gone.

To get rid of warts on a cow's udder, the first-born child of the family carefully counted the number of warts. He then took a wool thread that had hung in a milk pail a while and tied as many knots in it as there were warts, saying all the while, "I tie away your warts." The thread was then placed under a rock or clump of grass by the child, who was not allowed to turn around when walking away. When the thread had rotted, the warts disappeared.

Heugren reports from Appelbo several methods of stopping the flow of blood, based on transfer. A bleeding wound was a dramatic and serious event at the fäbod, one which required immediate attention. This urgency called forth many cures. Among those that Heugren mentions are: the tool or item that caused the cut was tied over the cut to absorb the evil. From Rääf, he reports a long list, including: during July, when the sun stands in The Lion, cut a branch off an ash at sundown with a new knife. When you want to stop the flow of blood, hold this stick with the left hand until the stick gets warm. Dip a sliver of wood from a bench or footstool in the blood and put the sliver back where it came from. Make birch sticks sharp pointed on one end and dip them in the blood and go to a wall and hit the sticks three time to drive them into a crack in the wall, saying "Here shall you stand."

THE USE OF CHARMS

Swedish archives and books are filled with long lists of different charms used in a variety of situations. I'll mention here a few that are connected with ailments and problems that occurred at the fäbod

To stop the flow of blood, a vallkulla could choose a variety of balms, physical methods, or combinations using charms. It is probable that, considering the seriousness of unchecked bleeding at the fäbod, they used all the combinations they could think of.

Granlund reports a charm to stop the flow of blood. One leaned over the cut and recited quietly three times without breathing:

> Stilla ska du stå
> som vattnet stod
> i Jordans flod
> når Jesus döptes
> igenom Faderns, Sonens,
> och den Helige Andens namn.
>> Still shall you stand
>> like the water stood
>> in the River Jordan
>> when Jesus was baptized
>> In the name of the Father,
>> Son, and Holy Ghost.

In this charm is a reference to a miracle that was said to have taken place when Jesus was baptized: the water in the river Jordan stopped running. This notion, writes Granlund,

> "comes from an apocryphal gospel that the church discarded and is lost to us, but whose statements reverberate in a Greek work from the early part of the 7th century, which records the more important data about Jesus's life. In translation, it says: 'And the Lord told John: order the river Jordan to stand still, for the Lord is among us.'"

"Amen" was never said, explains Granlund, since it was understood that if "Amen" was pronounced, one could not recite that charm over again for the patient, if it became necessary.

Granlund writes that two of his informants stressed that he should learn to see the difference between regular stopping the flow of blood and "last-recourse" methods for stopping bleeding. The latter is a very serious act. "You do it only when nothing else helps, but after you have done it, the blood will stop flowing from the wound. But if the blood starts to run from another cut at a later time, it is very difficult to stop it then."

To perform the "last-recourse" method, one should take flour that had been ground on a Sunday and, holding a shoe that had been repaired on a Sunday, put the flour on the wound, reciting:

Du ska stå så säkert
som de står i Helvete
som har malt detta mjöl
och lagat denna sko på söndan
   You shall stand securely
   as they stand in Hell
   who ground this flour
   and repaired this shoe on Sunday.

To do any kind of work on a Sunday was considered a great sin. To include a Sunday-made object in a charm is found only in Sweden, Norway, and Finland. Granlund does not offer an explanation, only asks the question: "Is the use of a Sunday-made object added in later years when the people felt that the power of the word alone was not sufficient?"

Charms played a curative roll in combination with many treatments, such as those above, but by themselves they were more protective than curative. For example, bees and wasps were common in the mountains. If one came near a vallkulla, it always helped if she stood absolutely still and chanted:

Geting, geting etterspik
av hin onde är du kommen, honom lik
Stick i mull, men ej i hull
stick i sten, men ej i ben
   Wasp, wasp, stinging needle,
   from the Devil do you come; are like him.
   Sting in the earth, not in the flesh
   Sting the stone, not the bone.

Charms were also used to treat snake-bite. There is one poisonous snake in the area, the viper. People seldom die from a snakebite, but some swell up badly. The cows can get very sick, depending on where they are bitten. One cure is described by Liss Anna in the ninth chapter, and there were also a variety of other cures—putting poultices or metal over the bitten area, drinking herb blends, or asking a "wise woman" (one especially skilled in folk cures) for help.

One snakebite charms went like this:

Du ormslok, som på tuva låg,
ett är tunga, ett är tand,
Jungfru Maria haver sagt
att det skall bindas och försvinna
som vattnet i en ström bortrinna.
You snake, that lay in the grass,
one part tongue, one part fang,
Virgin Mary has said
that it shall be tied up and disappear
as water in a stream runs off.

The Virgin Mary, of course, is not on record as saying any such thing about snakes, but the "author" of the charm seems to have felt she needed help, and so invoked the Holy image and its power.

"So many misconceptions about snakes existed that people were extremely frightened by them. The vallkullor would wear heavy wool stockings to protect themselves when they walked in a dry area where snakes were seen. They seldom dared run barefoot, even at the fäbod," explained Hjalmar Liss in Gagnef.

A sprained ankle or pulled ligament on cow or woman was attended to by application of an ointment and a charm recited three times. From Säfnäs comes the following cure for a sprain: Cut lines in fat with a knife and at the same time recite

Vår frälsare re
igenom ett le
hans häst vart vre
Han läste: ur vre och i le
Igenom Faderns, Sonens och
den Helige Andens namn.
Our Saviors rode
hurting a joint
his horse got a sprain
He read: Out, sprain, out!
In the name of the Father,
Son, and Holy Ghost.

Valeriana   **Daphne**

Now take the fat and rub it on the hurt leg from the top towards the hoof. It is best to burn the left-over fat."

Many illnesses were treated with a combination of cures. If a cow had eaten a sharp-edged or pointed object, one should give her a mixture of salt, shavings of brass, copper, and silver. If a cow, for example, had swallowed a needle (needles were sometimes stuck in the cow's neck chain to ward off trolls or Randa), it was believed that this mixture encased itself around the needle and prevented it from going to the heart. But most often, charms were recited to counteract the sharp objects in the cow's stomach: "Three maidens and two crossroads, all of them could measure. Sticks and steel, stone, bone, glass, brass, silver, gold, and all that is sharp shall destroyed be, in the name of the Trinity."

Many admonishing charms end with calling on the Holy Trinity as a counterpart to the evil that caused the ailment. This, writes Don Yoder,

"is based on the primitive world view of the unity of all things, heaven, earth, man, animal, and nature. Within this unity, there is a dualism between evil powers, concentrated in the Devil and his voluntary servitors, the witches, and good powers, concentrated in God, the Trinity, the saints, and the pow-wower who is the channel for healing power from sources to patient. Disease is believed to be demonic, 'sent' by evil forces into the person or animal, hence it has to be removed by a 'counterspell' which can be provided by ritual, written charms involving holy words, or prepared amulets."

A HARDY FOLK

Knowledge of plants for medical purposes was both common and mysterious. Some vallkullor excelled in the knowledge and were consulted as healers or "wise women." On the other hand, the folk stayed hardy with fresh air and exercise, and nothing much could get the better of their ingenuity. For example, Ida and Edit told how their grandmother had fallen and broken her leg at Osjöbuan in 1911. The old lady set the leg herself.

"She felt when it felt right. Grandma tied some wood sticks to her leg with baby swaddlings and stayed at the fäbod to the end of the summer, when she rode a horse home to the valley. Grandma's leg healed perfectly. She still walked the six miles to church way into her 80's. They were strong in those days.

"Grandma had eleven children and she never had any help delivering any of them. She used to say it wasn't difficult. She just stood on her knees when the baby arrived. And ten of the eleven children grew up to become adults. And not far from our fäbod is a flat area where a woman had a baby while walking up to the fäbod above us. The baby came rather quickly, so what could she do but stop? And when the baby was born, she wrapped it in her apron and walked on up to the fäbod."

Emma Södergren told how she helped her friend at Gillerbergets fäbod the summer of 1918. The cows had stopped to eat and her friend put her knitting in the bag and took out her knife to strip bark off a birch branch. A cow bumped into her from behind. She fell and the knife cut a deep gash in her hand. The blood spurted out and the tendon withdrew up into the arm. They had no first-aid material of any kind with them. Emma remembered that the lining of her heavy jacket was made of wool, so she cut a hole in the jacket and used the stuffing to put on the wound. She cut the lining into strips and wound them around her friend's hand. The knitting yarn was used to fasten the bandage. Higher up the arm, Emma tied her garter to lessen the flow of blood. The two girls walked back to the fäbod, where Emma cooked strong coffee for her friend, who was getting weak. With the help of the coffee and some visitors, the girl managed to walk the eight miles home to the village, where she found medical help.

CHAPTER TWELVE

FOLK BELIEFS

The beliefs, superstitions, and rituals that earlier so penetrated every-day life have survived to some extent into this century. Even today in Dalarna, particularly in the rural, culturally conservative areas, many people still explain that "Aunt Anna had seen Randa herself," or "She really believed in all that," or "Mother always greeted the gnome when she entered the barn."

The set of beliefs, superstitions and rituals that was a part of every-day life survived longer at the fäbod than in the villages. I think that beliefs that lay latent during the winter in the village, with all the family around, surfaced through environmental influences at the fäbod. The isolation and the deep, dark forests had their impact on the women's responses. The closeness of caves and cliffs brought the trolls and forest spirits closer, and, since such spirits were believed to be a threat to the cows, the vallkullor continued to keep up traditional beliefs and protective rituals much later than the people in the villages did.

COW-LORE

Since the cow was so important to the family's economy and survival, it is not surprising that a large part of fäbod folklore concentrated on the well-being of cows. Acts were performed to protect them from the forest beings, from getting lost, from attacks by bears and wolves. Other rites were performed to get a cow back if lost, to increase her milk supply, and so on.

The Peregrinus rite was performed to make the fäbod forest safe from wolves and bears. Peregrinus was the evil leader of the forest, and the beasts were his dogs. It was believed that these beasts had no power in an area where the noise of people could be heard. So, on May 16th, in Säfnäs and in Värmland, the province that borders Dalarna on the west, all the people in the village gathered in the evening, carrying anything that could make a noise—bells of all kinds, pots, pans, guns. Walking around in the forest, they made as loud and awful a noise as they possibly could, all the while screaming, "Peregrinus, tie up your dogs!" According to a tradition found only in Värmland, Peregrinus looked much like the Devil, with horns, hoofs, and a long tail. The people ended the evening by walking up to the top of a hill or small mountain and there lighting a bonfire.

The rest of the year, Peregrinus was not one of the forest spirits on people's minds. There are no legends about him, no tales in which he plays a part. He may have been connected only with the rite of May 16th. Knowledge of him seems to have disappeared when the danger of the beasts diminished, and the May 16th rites either disappeared or were absorbed into the rites of Valpurgis Night, April 30th, which involve the lighting of bonfires to drive away the spirit of winter. In the village of Ovanåker as late as the 1940's, for example, children used to tie bells on themselves in the afternoon of Valpurgis Night and run around the village, making as much noise as possible, having a lot of fun, without any knowledge of why they made the noise.

When the cows stepped outdoors for the first time each spring, a variety of acts were performed to protect them from evil spirits, to safeguard them from being stolen by the forest beings, to ensure that they would follow the bell cow, and to make them return to the fäbod each evening. Generally, these rites involved the threshold or the barn door.

During the 18th and 19th centuries, tar was considered to have magic power. A tar cross painted over the barn door would protect the cows all summer from the trolls. Tar crosses were also painted on the cows' backs and necks.

Steel was considered to have more power than tar and was used in a number of protective rites throughout the fäbod area. One of the most frequently performed seems to have been the placing of some-thing made of steel under or alongside the barn threshold, so that the cows had to step over it as they came out that first day. Axes or knives or a bit of broken scythe were used. Note that all these steel items have a sharp edge. A cross carved in the threshold with a steel knife was also protective. A straight pin fastened in the chain around the cow's neck protected her as long as the pin stayed in.

Mercury was also considered a very powerful protective agent. A small hole could be drilled in the barn's threshold and a few drops of mercury placed in it. After the cows and goats had stepped over it, evil beings could not come close to them.

Another group of rites performed on the first day the barns were opened have to do with ensuring that the cows would return home to the fäbod each evening. Variations of these acts were performed throughout the summer, on the way up to the fäbod, the first day there, etc.

At a farm in Malingsbo, for example, the lead cow's bell was filled with grass in the fall, which remained inside the bell throughout the winter. A bit of this grass was given each cow to eat as she stepped over the threshold for the first time in the spring. The cows would then follow the bell cow's bell home each night.

In Hartorp village, farmwives took the bell filled with grass and put it in the oven for a while first. Then it was stored in a little niche, just big enough for the bell, in the fireplace wall. This was done so that the cows would stay together and come home each evening when summer came, and not stay out in the forest.

Similar acts are reported from many areas. The lead cow's bell was filled with some or all of the following: grass, hay, chaff, flour, bread, salt, and scrapings from the bell or other metal. Each cow was given a pinch of this mixture from the bell as she stepped out the barn door and was told,

"Här får du en bit ur skälla,
sa du går hem till kvälla"
    (Here you get a pinch from the bell,
    so you'll go each eve to where you dwell).

This ritual of the bell, performed for each cow, was a wish to transplant in her a desire to belong with the bell, to follow the bell. In some areas, they added a few hairs off the bell cow's tail to strengthen the connection with the lead cow and her bell. This mixture was given in combination with the words, "**Som rumpan följer korna ska korna följer skälla**"(Just as the tail follows the cow, so shall the cow follow the bell).

Other items are also used in these transfer rites. Bumble-bees, for example, are known to be great homelovers, always returning at dusk. A desire to transfer this quality to the cows can be seen in the tradition of feeding the bell cow the very first bumble-bee seen in the spring. In Gagnef, the pea-vines were saved and given the cows to eat on Christmas Eve, not the first day out in the spring. The vines are intertwined and difficult to separate. When the farm wife gave her cows the pea-vines, she said "Now you shall hang together during the summer like the pea-vine hangs together."

One rite combines steel as the protective agent and bread mixed with something off the bell cow as the agent to ensure returning home. A pick axe was fastened over the barn door. A small cut was made in the tail of the bell cow and the blood dripped onto the corners that had been broken off three hard tack (rye bread) squares. The bread was then given the cows to eat.

To ensure the cows' well-being at the fäbod, a variety of acts were performed before starting the walk up to the mountains: some walked the cows three times counterclockwise around a boulder or rock stuck in the ground to increase the cows' desire to come back. A cross might be carved or painted over the threshold of the barn, in hope that passing the sign of the cross would protect the animals from all evil. The bell cow was often given a cross to wear in her neckband for a short while before leaving the village. Daphne and Valeriana could be tied onto the cows' neckbands, since (as an old proverb asserted) **"Tibast och vänderot, stå all ont emot"** (Daphne and Valeriana protect against all evil).

If wolves came too close during the walk up to the fäbod, it was said that if a farmer dropped the tying rope with its iron hook behind the wagon and let it drag on the ground, the wolves could not outrun the horses.

More acts were performed when they reached the fäbod. To protect the cows and goats from being stolen by trolls or other forest beings, many acts similar to those performed for the first day out of the barn were repeated as the cows stepped into the fäbod barn the first day: axes, knives, or other iron tools were placed so that the cows had to step over them; crosses were painted or carved over the door or on walls; Daphne and Valeriana were tied to the bell cow's chain; grass brought from the farm was put in the lead cow's bell and given each cow; and garlic could be hung in the barn to ward off the forest beings.

If Old-Lisa saw little red mushrooms growing at the fäbod, she knew that the **vittror** (the underground people) had been there before her. She therefore hung an old silver spoon in the barn as protection against the vittra-people, who otherwise would cause mischief to her cows and goats.

Different from these acts to ward off the forest spirits were the ones performed to ensure that the cows would come home and not wander off on their own in search of better grass or mushrooms. The cows could be led three times counterclockwise around a boulder next to the barn; the vallkulla could take a couple of hairs from each cow's tail and place them in the barn, making the cows want to return to "their missing piece." Or the vallkulla could make the cows fond of her, and thus want to return to her, by placing the bodice of her skirt alongside the threshold, so that the animals had to step over it, or she could take a piece of bread and hold it under her arm until it was soaked with

sweat and then give a bit of it to each cow to eat.

If a cow was lost, the vallkulla generally would have some idea about which direction a cow had disappeared and the search would begin there. But if she couldn't find the lost animal and didn't know which direction to turn next, she could throw a knife high up into the air and observe how it landed. The knife point would indicate the direction she should walk to find the lost cow. If a cow didn't come home, some vallkullor carefully dug up one of her footprints and turned it so it pointed toward the barn.

If the vallkulla met a rabbit while out searching for a lost cow, she might as well go home, because it was believed that you would not find the cow that day. The same held true if the birds stopped singing.

If a cow stayed out overnight, one could make her come home by performing this little ritual and reciting the charm.

> First, one must take a knife and carve three crosses in that threshold the cow last stepped over. Then, one must put the knife point in the center of the first cross and say, 'Now you shall come home, Star-bell' (or whatever the missing cow's name was). Move the knife point to the next cross and say, 'Now you must come home at once.' Finally, put the knife point on the last cross and say, 'Now you must come home today.'

"This always works, even if sometimes the cow doesn't come home until a few days later," explained Jubb Ingeborg.

One of her friends pointed out that

> "if one had a difficult cow who often stayed out overnight, one could 'promise' for her, and this always worked. We made a promise to give a pitcher of milk to the first poor person we met. If we didn't have any milk that was ours to give away, we used to promise to give a coin to the church."

In Gagnef, it was traditional for farmwives to pick special plants, mix them in the dough, and bake them in buns, which were given the cows to eat in the spring before they ate any fresh grass. The cows would then search for just these plants to eat during the summer.

From Malung, it is reported that the vallkullor took the cows up on a nearby hill before 5 a.m. on Midsummer Day to eat the dew, which was considered to have special powers for healing and ensuring good healthy life. That night, all the earth's power was concentrated in the dew. A silent agreement existed among the vallkullor that nobody took her cows to that hill before Midsummer.

Some traditions to get the cows to eat are of a more practical nature. The vallkulla could bang on a tree with her axe to make the cows believe that it was time to stop for lunch, since their vallkulla was chopping wood for the fire. From Lima, it is reported that the vallkulla should go around urinating, or pretending to, to make the cows stop walking and start eating.

COPING WITH SUPERNATURAL BEINGS

Most of the forests in northern Sweden are deep, dark, and can be overwhelming and mysterious. They provided a rich growing ground for a large variety of supernatural beings. Asa Nyman explains in her essay on supernatural beings and everyday superstitions that

"...the isolation, the tranquility suddenly broken by strange sounds or by a burst of bird cries or grinding of trees easily evoke fear, which activated the imagination. When one saw and heard things that couldn't be explained rationally, it was close at hand to interpret the unusual experiences as visions of the forest's own inhabitants: the trolls, the underground people, and so on."

In their backgrounds, the vallkullor in the fäbod area had beliefs in several supernatural beings: giants, huge pre-historic beings; trolls, ageless, collective beings, living in the mountains; vittra-people, invisible families of little people living underground; Randa, the beautiful lady of the forest; Näcken, the water spirit, luring people to drown; fairies dancing over the bogs; and ghosts crying in the night. This is not the end of the list, but I have selected the first four to discuss here, since they are more intimately connected with the fäbod lore than any other supernatural beings. I will also limit my discussion of these beings to their fäbod aspects and not the function they took on in other connections. Randa, for example, would be a sexual temptress to the logging men, whereas in the fäbod community she would steal cows and threaten the vallkullor with mischief.

THE VITTRA-PEOPLE

Of the supernatural beings, the vittra-people (the females are called **vittra**, the plural form is **vittror**) are most closely connected with the fäbod. They lived in families, underground, and were invisible, even when they were above ground. They were believed to look very much like ordinary people, except maybe a bit smaller. They marry, have children, get sick, laugh and cry, and die like the rest of us. In the fäbod area, they lived a fäbod life, with cows and goats, buföring, singing for their herds, and playing the herding songs. Their counterparts in the villages are called **vättar** and live a village life.

The vittra-people did not collect and hoard treasures, like the trolls, but they could, as a thank you for help, give a vallkulla a silver spoon or coin. Their choice of color in clothing was a sign of their mood; if a vittra dressed in white, she was happy, but if she dressed in red, she was angry. It was mostly the vittra women that interacted with people. The vittra-men were just there, seldom mentioned. Their clothing has been described in a few instances: a farmer's dark jacket with white knickers.

The vittra-people's cows were greatly admired and desired, for they were healthy, beautiful, fat, and gave endless amounts of milk. If a vallkulla got a vittra-cow in her possession by throwing a knife over her, she had to be careful how she milked her. Everything would be fine as long as she didn't take a new bucket when the one she was using was filled with milk, for if she did, the cow would give no more milk or die. In some areas, the vittra-cows are white; in other areas, white and red. In those areas, it was believed that the vittra-people hated black cows. But in other areas, the vittra-people were said to have black cows with golden horns. The vittra's bell cow had a bell with the most beautiful ring to it. Their goats were shining with health, their udders almost dragging the ground. And their horses could be heard; they ran in flocks and their hooves thundered in the ground. All the animals the vittra-people had were thus admired, for they had attributes greatly desired by people.

The vittra-people were not frightening, like ghosts, but just another kind of people who were friendly if treated politely and with consideration and if nothing was done to harm them. When they were friendly toward the vallkullor, they could help them, but, at the same time, they were unreliable, being invisible. One could irritate or anger them without knowing it. "Mother always greeted them when she stepped into the barn, and when she left she thanked them for the milk. She talked to them as if they were real people," said one woman.

Since the vittra-people lived underground, the vallkullor were careful to say "Move over" before they poured out water on the ground, or urinated, or lay down for a rest. If they neglected that, or in some other way irritated or harmed the vittra, they would become sick. The vittra-people bit the person in revenge. The vallkulla should then perform the "casting out" ritual (see chapter on Folk Medicine) or give something as a bribe at the place where she thought she was standing when she was bitten. If the vittra-person that bit one had died, there was no cure; one would die.

The vittra-people were believed to live in the fäbod cabins during the winter. Therefore many a vallkulla left a bit of food for them when she left in the fall, telling them goodbye and wishing them well. In the spring, she would greet them as she entered the cabin, giving them the dates for her stay. She had better stick to the departure date she had told them, or else they would seek revenge.

There are long lists of acts to perform to protect oneself and the animals from the mischief of an irritated vittra: don't imitate a vittra, don't make a lot of noise after sundown, don't build a fäbod across their buföring trail, don't neglect to put a coin in a corner when a new building is put up, and don't tell anyone about your encounter with a vittra-person until you have slept a night. As protection, the vallkullor performed many of the ritual acts described earlier in this chapter—use a leaf from the Bible or a hymn book, draw or carve or paint crosses, and use steel, glowing embers, Daphne and Valeriana.

There are several legends about vallkullor's interactions with the vittra-people, many of them of the migratory legends type known throughout Europe—assisting a vittra-women at the birth of her child, taking part in their weddings, etc. (See next chapter.)

RANDA, THE LADY OF THE FOREST

Gunnar Granberg has made a thorough study of Randa, a supernatural being who appears with different attributes throughout Sweden. She has many names—forest lady, forest ra, forest-Kari, Rånda, and Randa, to mention only a few. In the most southern province, Skane, where there are hardly any forests, she is a horse-spirit, but she changes to a lady as she enters the forest-covered provinces.

Her role changes according to the situation in which she appears: She brings good luck to a hunter who treats her well (here, she has the power over animals); she foretells weather; she lures people into the deep forests; she helps men who are making charcoal, often in exchange for sexual favors; she steals cattle from the vallkullor; and she seeks revenge if irritated or angered.

Randa is a raving beauty, tall with long, blonde, curly hair; she most often wears a green dress, but sometimes she is dressed in the local costume. She is most dangerous when she wears the local costume, for then she is out to steal a vallkulla's cattle.

There are two things that definitely set Randa apart from other women: she has no back, just a big hole, and she has a tail, which she hides or tries to hide under her skirt when she talks to humans. Carl von Sydow explains that this hole in the back stems from lonely woodsmen's erotic hallucinations: "When they lovingly wanted to put their arms around the lovely woman, they hugged only air, which naively was explained as a hole in her back."

In Randa's connection with the fäbod, sexual beauty is not present, but her mischievous, thieving acts are. She here takes on many of the attributes of a vittra-people, but she is different from them, in that she is a loner, does not have a family. Nor does she live underground, but rather in caves or crevasses in rocky cliffs.

Randa is a vallkulla in the respect that she owns cows and goats. She is heard singing and playing for them, and she moves her cattle between fäbod areas. She often has a dog with her, a shepherd's dog, which is curious, because only in one place, Sollerön, is it reported that vallkullor used dogs to help them with their herding.

Randa was both a threat and a help to the vallkullor. She tried to steal cows; but, at the same time, she could wake up a vallkulla if something was going wrong in the barn, or if she overslept. She then sang:

> Opp, symmengylta, och mjölka dina kor!
> Mina kor gå på grönevall,
> Dina få stå på lortepall,
> Och än sover du, symmengylta!

> > Up, sleepyhead, and milk your cows!
> > My cows are out in the green meadows,
> > Your cattle stand in dungpiles,
> > And you're still snoozing, sleepyhead!

Randa was known to sing and play horn exceedingly well. Many a vallkulla is said to have learned to sing or play from Randa by listening and imitating.

When people lost their way in the forest, it was believed that Randa or the trolls had led them astray and held them. Randa's beautiful laugh lured people deeper and deeper into the forests, until they no longer knew where they were. Many local legends dealt with this topic, and they, too, will be discussed in the next chapter.

The vallkullor protected their cows and goats from Randa in the same manner they protected cows against the vittra-people. Steel over or under the barn door or a cross painted above the barn door hindered Randa from entering. A newly delivered cow was protected by placing a knife above her or fastening a pin to the milk pail, or painting a cross of tar on her forehead, or cutting off her hair in the shape of a cross. The Lord's Prayer could be recited if the vallkulla thought her cows were threatened, or she could carry a leaf from the Bible or hymn book to ward off Randa's advances. A cross could be carved on the cow's neck chain, or a pin inserted there, or Daphne and Valeriana could be tied onto the chain.

TROLLS

The trolls live in large families in mountain halls. They vary a great deal in shape, size, and activities. In some tales, they are described as small; in others, they have borrowed the huge, super-human size of the giants. They dress in skins and furs, letting their hair and tails hang out. They dislike cleanliness, eat frogs, snakes, and grubs, and live to be hundreds of years old. They are not very bright, not very evil, but they certainly are clumsy. Rays of the sun or the sound of church bells kill them.

Carl von Sydow points out that

> "the vittra-people were considered to be close neighbors, living under the cabin or the barn, while the trolls lived further away, in a mountain —perhaps visible from the cabin, but still distant. One isn't suspicious or worried about close neighbors, but fear and suspicion more or less color the

relationship with the trolls, because of the wilderness and the distance to the mountains. Trolls have especially been blamed for the disappearance of people and cattle—who are said to be bergtagna 'taken into the mountains.' Troll babies have been exchanged for unbaptized infants."

The greatest threat from trolls was that they steal or kidnap people and animals. The protections against the trolls are the same as those used to ward off the vittra-people and Randa—steel, the sign of the cross, and other church-related acts, Daphne and Valeriana, fire. Per Erik Persson from Hamra (born 1865) explained that when he was young, he was taught to make a fire in the cabin as soon as they got to the fäbod in the spring. This fire would scare away the trolls. He lit a fire just before leaving in the fall, too, to keep the trolls away for the winter.

GIANTS

In the folk beliefs of Dalarna, giants belong to a time long ago, since which they have died out. They are present in many tales that explain natural phenomena. A huge rock in the middle of a flat field was said to have been thrown there by a giant who was trying to hit the church. Huge crevasses or caves were said to have been dug by the giants.

The distinction between giants and trolls has grown less clear with time. The belief that giants lived in specific mountains stayed on, but the giants have shrunk with time and become more troll-like.

The vittra-people, trolls, and Randa are substituted for each other, depending on location. In some areas, it is said that the vittra-people do their buföring on Thursdays, while in other areas it is the trolls or Randa who are moving their cattle. I heard one interesting comment from a child of today, who did not know about Randa. When one is sitting on a mountain slope in the evening and sees steam rising up from bogs and lakes, it used to be said that Randa was cooking her whey-butter; the younger generation has changed that to "The foxes are cooking whey-butter." Each according to his knowledge!

HALLUCINATION?

Carl von Sydow has discussed the circumstances that helped develop belief in forest beings and the events that have sustained these beliefs. He points out that hallucinations, illusions, and dreams are natural phenomena and can be perceived and understood as reality; and that they are interpreted in accordance with a person's associations and awareness of traditions. As an example of how the tradition of Randa could have been created, he points to her in the role as temptress.

"When mostly men are working in the forest, it is natural that erotic fantasies are expressed in female hallucinations.

The loneliness of the forest is a growing ground for suc-
cubus experiences. When it became clear that it was not a
real woman the men had associated with, they concluded
that a supernatural female lived in the forest."

Randa becomes an association center, which attracts everything
else unexplainable in the forest: she and her beautiful, luring laugh are
blamed if one gets lost in a supposedly familiar forest—that is, one
picks an external, rather than an internal, reason. She is blamed for
bad luck in hunting, because the hunter is reluctant to accept the fact
that he is a bad shot or unskillful. She is blamed if a cow is lost; and so
on. In areas where she dominates as an association center, she is
immediately thought of as an explanation for the unexplainable. When
the vallkulla oversleeps and is awakened by a knock (it could have
been a tree branch blown against the cabin, or even a distant noise in
the forest or fäbod), the vallkulla, feeling guilty at oversleeping, is more
apt to explain the knock as Randa's than to use a clear head and
accept the responsibility herself.

A person who had been lost for days in the forest and succeeded in
returning home must have had hallucinations and dreams, because of
hunger and exhaustion, suggests von Sydow. He or she returns to a
village where people expect that the trolls or Randa had kidnapped
him, so he interprets his experience in accordance with the association center that dominates locally. When a baby suddenly acts up and
cries or is writhing from high fever, it is easier to say the trolls had
exchanged this fussy baby of theirs for the human baby—to seek an
external explanation—than to examine the real fault. When a cow
suddenly begins to give less milk, the vallkulla remembers hearing of
the vittra-people's tendency for revenge and uses that as a close-at-
hand explanation, rather than trying to find out if, for example, the cow
had eaten something that didn't agree with her.

Dreams and hallucinations are more common among people living
on the borderline of starvation than for us today. Maybe their imagina-
tions were livelier and quicker than ours, too. They could dream that
they heard or saw a person in the room, then discover upon awaking
that no one was there and the doors and windows were closed; it is
then easy to conclude that it must have been some supernatural
being. The quick disappearance is taken as proof of the supernatural,
simply because no real person can disappear that quickly. Thus, a
fund of accumulating personal experiences, retold through the generations, kept alive the belief in the vittra-people, Randa, and the trolls.

The vallkullor, isolated, a bit lonely at times, scared at other times,
lived with the supernatural as neighbors. Asa Nyman explains in an
article,

"Even in recent Swedish traditions, there are uncount-
able numbers of stories about how someone had heard,

seen, or otherwise felt the presence of vittra-people and other supernatural beings. If today's storytellers themselves believe that (a supernatural event) really happened, or if they tell it only to entertain, is unclear. One comes probably closer to the truth if one conceives of it as a kind of half-belief, a latent belief, which can surface with greater or lesser strength during special circumstances, or within persons inclined toward it.

THE DEAD CHILDREN

Another category of supernatural beings connected with the fäbod area, but separate from the vittra-people, Randa, and the trolls, is the ghosts of murdered babies. Tales of such babies are found throughout Scandinavia; however, as Pentikainen points out, "compared to other Swedish provinces, Dalarna has a special position as far as dead-child beings are concerned, in that nowhere else are there items about so many different beings. . . . There are altogether six dead-child names in Dalarna:"

It is natural that legends about unwed mothers murdering their new-born babies would flourish in the fäbod area, since the threat of pregnancy was very real for many vallkullor and since they could give birth in secret, taking advantage of their isolation. It would take only a couple of actual cases to spur the growth of such legends. Some court records from the 18th century prove that just such events did take place.

The **utkastning** "outcast"—a placeless dead-child being—is more heard than seen. These outcasts cry or whimper in the night in the fäbod or near the place where they are suspected of being buried. To quiet such a ghost-baby, one could give it a silver coin, but not with the hand, for then one's hand would be broken. One had to split a stick, put the coin in the crack, and leave it where the cry was heard. Ghost-babies were believed to cry as long as they would have lived normal lives, or until they have announced who the mother was. A number of folk rhymes are these babies' announcements:

Byttan är trang	The box is short
Bena är lang	The legs are long
Kari äg ma	Kari owns me.

OFFERING PLACES

Along some trails leading up to fäbodar, one still can find offering places. These are usually places distinguished by some remarkable natural phenomenon, such as a deep crevice in a rock, a circular hole in a flat rock, or a rock with some odd shape. The most often reported gifts laid in these places were not coins, but rather items from nature, such as a green twig from a tree or bush, pine or spruce cones, or pebbles.

In Orsa County, there was an "offering pile" of sticks and branches, which had been put there by people on their way up to the fäbod. The idea was that they would not grow tired of walking if they gave up a symbolic walking stick at that place.

Tegengren believes that these gifts were offered to Randa (who lives in rocks), so she would not steal their cows. They might also have asked Randa for help in producing as much milk and milk-products as possible.

It was important that, when a vallkulla threw a pebble or branch, it landed inside the hole or crevice in the rock. At one place, they were supposed to throw in as many pebbles as they had cows—if a pebble fell outside, they would lose a cow that summer. Into other offering places were thrown pine cones, or pebbles, while saying "I give the poor a penny." This would bring good luck with the cows. Lars Ahs from Älvdalen offers an interesting bit of information, recorded in 1930:

> "At the fork in the road to Rälldalen, where the trail takes off to Baltzars fäbod, a tree stump has stood as long as anyone can remember, dressed in a skirt, sweater, kerchief, and with a bag, all of Älvdalen's design. In the bag are a pipe made of iron, matches, knife, tobacco, and a few copper coins. When, in recent years, the tree stump began to totally disintegrate, it was replaced by a thick post set deeply in the ground, which was dressed in the same clothes. It is called the Baltzar maiden and is still attended to.

> "The beliefs behind this custom are not totally explicable, but we think that this is an age-old offering place, where people offered gifts for the welfare of their cattle. It was the lady of the forest they had to please. It is not impossible that the place is an offering place from pre-Christian days, when the Rälldals road was the road to Härjedalen and on to Norway. The travellers gave offerings to the forest spirits, particularly Randa, to ensure a successful journey through the deep dark forests.

> "According to old traditions, female spirits ruled the forests. It was natural then, that the people on the way to the fäbod wanted to seek (Randa's) protection for their animals. She could protect them from wolves and bears and keep them from getting lost in the forest. Anders Tiger was out searching for cows that had been lost for weeks. He passed this statue, broke off a green branch, and placed it in front of the statue. Just a little while after that, he met all his cows, right in the middle of the trail."

PROVERBS AND SAYINGS

An abundance of proverbs and proverbial sayings exist in Sweden, but only a few are directly connected with fäbod life.

A number of these folk sayings are connected with the weather. "If it rains in the open book, it'll rain all week" refers to the Bible, which was opened outdoors on Sundays at fäbod church services. "If the cows shake and stiffen their back legs while shitting, bad weather is coming." "When the cows shake themselves, snow flurries are coming." "If the cows lie down back to back, there will be a change in the weather." If someone got soaking wet in a rainstorm, they said "**Han ar vat som en vallkulla**" (he is as wet as a vallkulla).

Some of these local proverbs and sayings are connected with the sexual morals and behavior of the vallkullor and their boyfriends. When a boy started staying overnight at some fäbod, it was said, "**Han börja a ligg borta som Backolles kur**" (he has begun to sleep away from home, like Backolle's cows). If a vallkulla returned from the fäbod pregnant, it was said, "**Sommarhullet stanna kvar**" (her summer-fat stayed on). A saying about fidelity was more involved. The berries of the juniper bush take three years to ripen; thus each bush always has new, half-ripened, and ripe berries all at once. People said,

Det år all enbuskens bär blir mogna
Är alla flickor gifta och trogna.
That year when every juniper berry is ripe
Every girl will be married and faithful.

There is a long list of "if you do this, then ..." sayings, which reflect folk beliefs.

If a brown cow gets a black calf, someone will die.
If the cows bellow without reason, an accident will happen.
If you spill milk, the cow will get sores on her udder.
If you sit on a tree-stump, the cows will not walk home.
If you prevent a cow from entering the barn (if she comes home too early), she'll come to hate the barn.
If you tell about seeing Randa, without first sleeping one night, you'll get sick.
If you imitate the vittra-people, you'll get very ill.
If the cows are tired and huffing and puffing in the morning, the trolls have ridden them.
If the cows are walking loose and milked in the morning, Randa has been there.
If the whey-butter boils heavily in the center, visitors will be coming to the fäbod.
If the cows all lie on the same side, visitors will come.
If you make a racket with the buckets after nightfall, the troll's dog will come, bringing unhappiness.

If you make tools of birch branches on Fridays (the day Jesus was crucified), an accident will happen.

FOLK BELIEFS SURFACED AT THE FÄBOD

It's really difficult to find out to what extent folk beliefs and superstitions lived on at the fäbod into this century. The isolation, the often mysterious disappearance of cows or a change in their behavior, the necessity of dealing with difficult tasks, often accompanied by unexplained happenings or noises in the forest, all encouraged the vallkullor to accept the traditional folk beliefs as reasonable explanations. As Liss Anna said,

"When it was getting dark and I had to go out looking for the cows, I started to wonder if maybe it wasn't true, after all, all those things Trum-mor had told me about Randa. By the time I got to the creek and saw those glowing eyes, I was sure it was Randa."

Another old vallkulla, who prefers to remain anonymous, said about her years as a young vallkulla,

"There were a lot of things we didn't think about during the winter, for they sort of belonged to the fäbod. When you are up there in the fall and it rains and gets very dark, you get kind of pensive about it. While you are in the village, you know that Randa does not exist, but up there you are not so sure any longer. You sort of believe and don't believe at the same time.

"Kari, one of the older women at the fäbod, used to tell vividly about how she had seen Randa. She explained in detail how Randa looked and exactly where she had met her. Kari really believed in Randa. And was she ever scared of the dark! Evenings, we could hear how she sang hymns to calm herself. We didn't like her very much and, one time, we played a joke on her, which was awful, because she got really scared. We had been out visiting and were walking home to our fäbod late one evening. Just as Kari walked off toward her cabin, one of us asked her, 'Did you see that lady dressed in white, out there on the bog?' Kari panicked and got really mean."

The vallkullor I interviewed had an easier time talking about how they made cheese than talking about trolls, Randa, or the vittra-people. It is even more difficult to reach any kind of understanding about how much magic and ritual was used and how late, since these were really looked down upon in the village from the end of the last century. It seems safe to say, however, that the fäbod experience called forth a kind of half-belief, which persisted right up to the end.

CHAPTER THIRTEEN

TALES AND LEGENDS TOLD AT THE FÄBOD

Around the turn of the century, when all-day herding was no longer necessary, the vallkullor had more time for socializing. They gathered around the fire in one cabin and told stories and sang while they knitted. The older vallkullor, especially, told the younger ones about strange events they had been involved in, or things they had heard others tell about, stories about vallkullor's encounters with bears and wolves; tales about Randa; about the troll's dog, whose muffled bark sounded strange in the lonely mountains; about tricky trolls whose thoughts were always on mischief; about the water spirit who played his fiddle in the creek; about the mysterious, deep-forest lakes. As Gustav Dalmalm has remarked, "There was adventure and excitement in these tales and legends, while the fire burned down and the red embers were reflected in the small squares of the cabin windows. Outside, one perceived odd beings move in the dark fall evenings."

Storytelling was certainly more common at the fäbod than in the village. "Oh, those women!" exclaimed Lilly Sterner-Jonsson,

> "Never did one hear them say a word about these things when they were at home with their realistic and down-to-earth extended family. Then they sat in their corner with their work, quietly, speaking at most about a new calf, the weaving, flax preparations, and such. But at the fäbod, where they were sent with the older children and maybe a young girl they were to teach to become a vallkulla, there they blossomed. Oh, how they could tell stories!"

When I visited Lilly Sterner-Jonsson, she went on at length:

"When the evening came and the work was done, we sat down by the open fireplace and cooked the porridge. After we had eaten, we picked up our knitting. When I grew up, it was grandma that went up to the fäbod. She took the grandchildren along to help her and to keep an eye on them. Also it got us out of the way of all the work that had to be done on the farm. At the fäbod, the other women came to grandma's cabin in the evenings with their knitting, and they sat there telling stories. Sometimes, we were told to go to bed when the tales got too scary, or when ghost stories were told. But we didn't go to sleep. We lay there very still, pretending to sleep, and listened to all those scary stories.

"They told of old, old events and of things that had happened during their younger days and earlier. It was seldom about their own experiences, as it was rather difficult to get them to talk about themselves, but it was events that had happened in the area to friends, or legends like 'Tulleri Tova, Twelve Men in the Forest,' for example. They sang that one and told the story behind the song.

" 'Tulleri Tova' was about a vallkulla that was alone at the fäbod. She had been attacked by twelve outlaws. She managed to get away from them, carrying her horn with her. She blew the warning melody that they used if a bear was attacking. You see, the bear was called 'twelve-man,' since they didn't want to call him by his name. Which is oldest, the warning melody for bears or the song about the twelve outlaws, I don't know. When the vallkulla blew that melody, the people in the valley knew she needed help, and they came up and rescued her and killed all twelve outlaws. They are buried on an island here in Lake Siljan somewhere. They have found human bones on that island. But, on the other hand, that same story and song is found in many places in northern Sweden and in Norway, too; so one really can't say what's behind the story, or where it really happened, or if it did.

"I heard many other tales at the fäbod. One of them was 'The Girl who Stepped on the Bread.'. A young vallkulla whose name was Kersti was working as a maid to a family in Limån. It was a good family she worked for. She was both pretty and a good worker, so she was liked very much. When Midsummer arrived, she was given some time off to go home. She knew that her parents were not on their farm on Sollern, but at their fäbod, Borrberg. Her kind employer had given her a new pair of shoes with some layers of birch bark on the soles, and she was careful with her new shoes. She was also given two cakes of bread, which she put in a kerchief and carried in her hand. She walked along the old buföring trail, by way of Överåsen and Solleråsen, and passed Björnmyren towards Björka. From there she took the trail towards Lövbergbron (a bridge), but before she got to the river, the trail crossed a creek. There the creek flows slowly, so there was a lot of mud where the trail crossed the creek. She stood there and looked from the mud to her new shoes, which she just that morning had scraped so that the bark layers in the sole shone so white and beautifully. How was she to get across without getting her new shoes dirty?

"Her eyes fell on the bundle with the bread inside. If she put it in the creek, it would surely float, and the kerchief would protect the bread, and then she could step over ever so lightly. But wasn't the bread a loan from God? And wasn't it a sin to step on a loan from God? She didn't hesitate very long. She threw the bundle in the mud and stepped out as softly as she could. The bread bundle sank about an inch and then slid away, and she sank in the mud. She fought against the mud with all her might, but it was as if an invisible hand from the depth pulled her deeper and deeper down into the mud. Soon her frantic calls were silenced. Only the bread bundle lay there, as a silent reminder that something horrible had happened.

"That bread bundle that floated on the mud was also the only thing they found when they started searching for the girl. But the one who never stopped searching was the girl's mother. Each Midsummer Night, she walked to the creek where Kersti had disappeared and called, 'Kersti, Kersti mine, Kersti mine. Are you mine?'

"It is said that she had heard Kersti crying to her from the bubbling depth of the creek. Her mother never stopped hoping. Out of the mother's own heart came, 'One day when the soil's crops once again have been blessed, Kersti will have paid for her sin, and then the creek will let go of her. Faith will be the ladder on which Kersti can climb up out of the grip of the creek and continue walking the trail her mother has walked, and Kersti can once again come home to the summer-green Borrberg fäbod.' "

I've heard many variations of that tale, but it always seems to use local place names wherever it is told.

"Sometimes it happened that a vallkulla was alone at a fäbod, and that was a rather taxing time. In the fall evenings, harder winds rattled the buildings and the animals stirred outside. Fright was not far off then, and it could play tricks on a woman. She would often have odd thoughts those nights. A friend of mine who usually doesn't believe in anything supernatural told me of an incident that happened when she was a child. She was thirteen or fourteen years old and working at the Gotland fäbod. One day, a strange cow came to the fäbod and hung her head over the fence. She stood like that, just looking at them. She was really very shy and skittish. Slowly, they managed to talk to her and finally she allowed them to pet her, but she just wouldn't let them come close enough to milk her. Finally, they got her into the barn. They slept in the hay loft above the barn. At midnight, they heard the cow bellow so strongly that all three of them awoke. They didn't think much of it and, since they were very tired, they soon fell asleep again. But in the morning, when they climbed down, the cow was gone. Her chain was still locked and the door was closed. They asked all over, and even in the Leksand area, but no one had lost a cow. Where did that cow come from and where did she go? Can anyone explain that?"

Lilly Sterner-Jonsson is involved in gathering and recording on tape many of the tales that were told at the fäbodar at the beginning of this century. She is beginning to believe that local legends were told most often and that the wonder tales were not as popular as she had once expected.

BEARERS OF FOLKTALES

Some women were better at telling stories than others, of course. Their lyrical talent differed remarkably. It is reported that some injected a poetic tone into the stories they told, some were able to create a fascinating atmosphere, some were elegant in their word-choice. But, in the village, they were passive carriers of the tales; they blossomed into active storytellers only at the fäbod.

Carl von Sydow developed the theory of active and passive bearers of folktales. Active bearers are those who actually tell the tales; passive bearers are those who listen to the performances, who know the tales, but who do not retell the story or legend. The women Lilly Sterner-Jonsson talks about are beautiful examples of von Sydow's concept that the circumstances determine if a person becomes an active teller of tales, or if she, knowing the tales well enough to tell them, chooses not to tell them, or perhaps defers to a more clever tale-teller. The vallkullor were both active and passive bearers, according to the season of the year. Von Sydow saw the shift from passive to active only when, for example, a person moved and settled in a new area, or if the active bearer in the community died. Then a passive bearer might begin actively telling the stories he knew. But the vallkullor

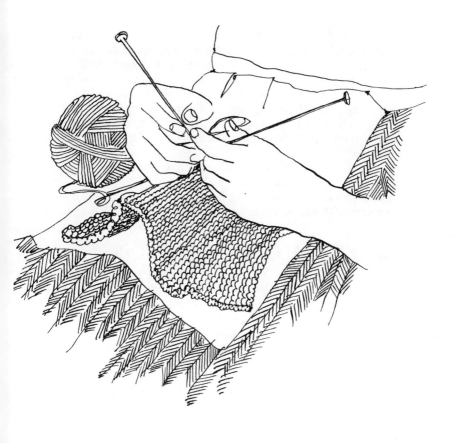

switched back and forth between these roles, alternating as surely as the seasons themselves.

The stories the vallkullor told were mostly local legends, or migratory legends that had taken on local place names and characters. Tales of the **Märchen** type (wonder tales) seem not to have been very popular. Even wonder-tales about trolls and giants were given geographical location in the area and put in a local time perspective. Thus they take the core of the wonder-tale, but the dimension of a local legend. Most of the local legends are far less fabulous than the wonder-tales, which are set in the never-never land of fairies, monsters, and magic. But some legends, in particular the migratory legends that had taken on a local flavor, were told by skillful vallkullor in a style and length close to the wonder-tales.

In his background discussion of Swedish folktales, John Lindow says of migratory legends:

> "What makes them migratory is the fact that, like wonder-tales, they exist in several variants, widely diffused in time and space. This suggests a definite geographic and temporal development for each of these migratory legends; in the case of Scandinavia, nearly all must have come from the south. It should be stressed, however, that once a legend has been accepted locally in a given tradition, it may become quite localized; that is, it may be told as having happened to a person known to the tradition-bearers in a place known locally to them."

Many of the local fäbod legends describe interactions between vallkullor and supernatural beings. Others deal with lost cows, dead children, extreme illness, attacks by bears or wolves. There are at least nine groups of these legends, which can be illustrated with a few examples.

1. LEGENDS ABOUT VITTRA-PEOPLE

Since the vittra-people lived a fäbod life, it is not surprising that there are a very large number of legends about vallkullor and vittra-people. One of the more popular ones tells about the problems a vallkulla had with a young vittra-man who wanted to marry her. The vallkulla was alone at her fäbod. Every evening, the young vittra-man would come to her, proposing marriage, but she always refused. When the vallkulla's mother came up to fetch the cheeses and butter, the girl told her of her problem with the vittra-man. Her mother contacted the young vittra-man's mother and asked her, "What can I do? Your bull is very much interested in one of my cows, but she does not want to have anything to do with him. How can I stop his advances?" The vittra-woman answered, "Take Daphne and Valeriana, and hang them around her neck, and then he can't come close. Daphne and Valeriana ward off all evil". So the vallkulla's mother took a bit of each plant and put them in a little bag, which she hung around her daughter's neck. And from that day on, she was never again bothered by the young vittra-man.

The vittra-mother got very angry when she discovered she had been tricked, but there was nothing she could do. She called out in anger, "**Tibast och vänderot stå allt ont emot. Stor tok jag var som gav dig bot.**" (Daphne and Valeriana ward off all evil. Big fool was I to teach you the cure.)"

Since the vittra-people were invisible, the vallkullor had to be very careful not to bother or irritate them. There are many legends describing accidental encounters. In one, a barn had to be moved because it was built over the vittra living quarters. The vallkulla was invited underground to see how urine from the barn ran down on the vittra table, and she agreed that the barn had to be moved.

These legends can be very short, a mere anecdotal description: "We sat down to eat our lunch on a big flat rock that was called the Vittra-stone. It was her table. As punishment, she sent a bad rainstorm."

People had to be very careful not to block the vittras' roads or buföring paths either. One legend about imposing upon the terri-tory of the vittra-people comes from Ljusbodarna:

Up at Ljusbodarna, an old vallkulla was cutting grass on a marshy slope. Toward evening, she stacked her grass in neat piles and went home. But she had put the stacks in the middle of the vittra-people's road. She didn't know where these invisible roads were. The next morning, the vallkulla got really dismayed when she got back to her haying area. All the grass was strewn out over a large area, and all her work was for nothing. But she got yet another surprise. She found a lot of small sticks—she told me they were about a half-yard long—among the cut grass. She realized something odd was going on. She figured out that the vittra-people must have their road just there. She was thankful they hadn't taken a worse revenge than they had, because she knew from the older vallkullor's tales that those whom the vittra-people sought revenge against could become very sick for a long time. So, happy and thankful, she began to rake her grass together again. This time, she placed the stacks of grass way off.

When the vallkullor from Gräsberget's fäbodar stopped for lunch on Halvar's Hill, they did not dare to start eating until they had asked, "May we stay?" three times in a row. If they didn't, their cows would not settle down and rest. One Midsummer Night, a vallkulla came to that spot while out searching for her cows that hadn't come home. She found there on the ground a pile of jewelry of gold, silver, and copper. They were so heavy she could not lift one of them. In order to find the place again, she hung her cap on a bush. When she returned with her friends to help her, there hung caps on every bush. She pulled one of the caps off a bush, and then every cap disappeared. She just stood there, knowing nothing.

Another cautionary tale tells of a vallkulla who woke up one night and saw that the vittra-people were using her cabin to hold a wedding. She lay very quietly in her bed, observing the feast, but when the bride suffered a mishap, the vallkulla broke out laughing. Everybody disappeared at once. Later, on her own wedding day, the vallkulla suffered the same mishap as the vittra-bride. It was the vittra's punishment for her laughing at them.

Another legend about the vittra-people's revenge comes from a fäbod just north of Dalarna.

The men had gone up to the fäbod Tjärnbuan to repair fences. The evening arrived and everybody had gone to bed. The open fire had burned down and its fading embers left a twinkling twilight in the cabin.

Suddenly, the door opened and some vittra-people walked into the room and started to putter around. One old vittra-man walked up to the foot end of uncle's bed and leaned over it as if he was about to jump in. Since uncle was not particularly pleased with the idea of such a bedfellow, uncle delivered a terrible kick to the old vittra-man. The kick was so strong that the old vittra-man tumbled into the fireplace. Embers and ashes whirled into the room, and the old vittra-man remained lying in the fireplace.

Now a terrible confusion broke out among the vittra-people. They took the old vittra-man from the fireplace and carried him out. Outside, in the yard, a lot of crying and complaining could be heard, "Grandpa is dead, Grandpa is dead." A lot of commotion could be heard, creaking harnesses, ringing cowbells, bellowing cows, and bleating of goats. The sound moved further and further away, until it no longer could be heard. The vittra-people moved and, after that night, they were never again seen at Tjärnbuan's fäbod.

The men in the cabin hurriedly gathered up the glowing embers and the hot ashes. The tar-wood floor had begun to catch on fire, here and there.

When they had gotten most of it cleaned up, uncle said, "That old vittra-man bit me on my big toe!"

In the light from the fire they had started in the fireplace, everyone could now clearly see deep cuts from the old vittra-man's teeth. To clean the cut and stop the flow of blood, uncle poured eldsmörja, a mixture of fresh butter and soot, on his cuts, as that was the usual way to treat cuts in those days.

The toe kept on aching and got more and more infected, till gangrene sat in, and uncle died. It was considered to be the revenge of the vittra-people.

This event took place sometimes in the 1830's. The old people told that they had heard it from the ones that were present at the cabin that night. Everyone insisted that all those present had seen and heard the whole event. The cabin was torn down sometime in the 1870's. The rather deep-burned holes in the floor were proofs of what had happened.

The teller assured the collector, E. J. Lindberg, in 1962, that the event really took place. But since the cabin no longer stands, we'll have to take his word for it.

Vittra-people could also be friendly and helpful to the vallkullor, as many legends show. One of them tells of a little girl who had a vittra-child as a playmate. But the day the girl told her mother about her playmate, it disappeared. Another legend tells of how a vittra-woman taught a vallkulla how to tie a cow's neck-chain of birch branches in a cross-like fashion, and if she tied it just right she would never be without milk. Both these tales, of course, express deep human wishes.

Other tales relate how vittra-women woke the vallkulla when her whey-butter was about to boil over, or when a cow was in danger. Järkers Kerstin told about how she had been sound asleep when a vittra-woman came and woke her up, telling her that a cow was about to strangle herself. Kerstin ran out to the barn and found that one of her cows had become tangled in her chain and had fallen down, so she was about to hang herself. Had she not arrived just then, her cow would have died.

Since the vittra-people had what the vallkullor so wanted—fat, beautiful cows that supplied endless amounts of milk—there are many legends about phantom cows. The vallkulla hears a cow, but when she gets to the spot where the sound seems to be, the sound has moved further on and continues to move further on. The vallkulla is never able to find that cow. If a vallkulla managed to find a vittra-cow, she could make it hers by throwing a knife or axe over it.

There are almost countless legends about persons who have heard the vittra-people, heard their buföring, their beautiful singing, and their cows' bells. All of them are offered as proof that the vittra-people exist. Many of these legends even give exact names, dates, and places.

Where did the vittra-people come from? There are four explanatory legends, all connected with the Bible.

One of these legends is based on the belief that there had been, originally, seven Books of Moses. Books six and seven had been removed from the Bible by the priests when people began to learn to read, because the populace would be impossible to manage if they read these last two books, for they contained the secret sciences, writings about vittra-people, trolls, Randa, gnomes, ghosts, magic, charms, and spells. It was believed that only one Bible in the world contained these two books—the Wittenberg or black Bible. In the missing books, it was explained that Adam had been married once before he married Eve. His first wife was Lucia, but there was one thing wrong with her: she had the same reproductive organs as animals, and thus she was led by her urges and instincts to give birth to several children every year. God realized Lucia was unfit to be the ancestress of mankind. Were all women to inherit her instincts and fertility, the world would soon be an utter, confused mess. God therefore sent Lucia to live underground, invisible until the day of judgment. Her offspring became the vittra-people.

Other explanatory legends mix up Lucia and Eve. God came to visit Adam one day. His children were very dirty. In some tales, Adam is married to Lucia, in others to Eve. The wife hurries and washes the children as God is approaching, but she doesn't have time to wash them all. She hides the unwashed children. God asks her if she has any more children than the ones he sees. She says, "No." "Then that's the way it shall be," says God, and he made the hidden, unwashed children of Adam invisible. They were the ancestors of the invisible vittra-people.

In another legend, Adam is married to Drucilla before Eve. She was as strong as Adam and wanted to rule over him. This infuriated God, but he pardoned her twice. The third time she tried to rule over Adam, God wanted to kill her, but pardoned her instead and made her invisible. She was pregnant at the time and bore invisible children, who became the vittra-people.

Carl von Sydow points out yet another explanation for the vittra-people. Those angels that remained neutral when Lucifer was thrown into hell were saved and landed on earth—in waters, mountains, forests, and underground. Thus all trolls, elfs, Randa, the vittra-people, etc., were created.

2. LEGENDS ABOUT RANDA

The legends depicting the vallkullor's encounters with Randa are very similar to the legends about encounters with vittra-people. Like the vittra-people, she keeps cows and goats, steals the vallkulla's animals, and does forest mischief. Sometimes she is friendly and helpful, but usually she is evil. Protective rituals against Randa often involve steel, Daphne and Valeriana, verbal charms, and invocations of Bible or hymn book.

Perhaps Randa's most common act is stealing cows. If a cow was missing, for example, Randa could be blamed as easily as the vittra-people. If the vallkulla found the cow standing motionless, she assumed the cow was under Randa's power. By throwing a knife over the cow, the vallkulla broke the spell, and the cow could walk home.

Another legend shows Randa in her aspect as a trickster. A vallkulla hears a strange cow near the fäbod and goes out to fetch it. But when she gets to the place where she heard the cow, the cow has moved further away. She follows, and again the cow moves further away. This goes on until the vallkulla is lured far from the fäbod and she realizes it must be Randa's cow. When she turns around to walk home, the cow's bellowing stops.

Randa also has several other kinds of behavior. Some legends depict how angry Randa becomes if she has forgotten to hide her tail under her skirt and someone mentions it. Sometimes, Randa is in a trading mood. In one legend, for example, she offers several goats for one of the vallkulla's cows, and the deal is made. Other legends describe how fast Randa can move. In one instance, she is heard singing nearby, and in the next moment she is far up the hillside. Short little tales of persons who have met or heard Randa are almost countless; they often give exact names and places. For example:

Nissliss Anders and Finsk Jan were on their way home from having watched the courting of the capercaille (a wild bird about the size of a turkey). Near Lindfäbod, they heard a lot of cow bells. By the time they got to the bog, they heard the vallkulla calling to her cows, and the herd was coming closer and closer. But it was winter and, of course, no vallkullor could be in the forest at that time. The calls and the sound of the bells got very close to the trail the men were on. Suddenly, it got absolutely quiet, but then the sounds started up again on the other side of the trail. The men never saw either vallkulla or cows cross the trail. They listened until the sounds vanished toward Kottle mountain.

On occasion, Randa could be helpful, too. "Kvarsve Kari was walking in the forest, searching for her lost cows, some time during the 1880s. Next to a huge rock sat a woman rocking a baby in a cradle and singing 'Kari, Kari, the cows are near the bog, Kari.' She went to the bog, and all her cows were standing there."

3. LEGENDS ABOUT TROLLS

Inside the fäbod area, trolls have a slightly different personality from the ones living outside the area. To the vallkullor living in the forest, the trolls were neighbors and much more closely related to the vittra-people and Randa than in the rest of Sweden, where trolls appear only in wonder-tales. Trolls in fäbod area tales are associated with specific locations and interact with persons that are named. They borrow from the vittra-people and Randa a way of life also: they are a herding people with cows and goats; they steal the vallkulla's cows; they move from fäbod to fäbod, etc.

"The Troll Wedding at the Fäbod" is by far the best known and studied of the troll legends. There are a large number of variants of this legend, which adapts readily to the place it is told. Different recorded versions place the wedding at Breds and Döderåsens fäbod in Älvdalen county, at five different fäbodar in Mora county, four in Orsa, and so on. Most specific of all the locations is a fäbod in Äppelbo that got its name from the legend, **Brudskogens fäbod** ('Bride's-forest' fäbod), which was exhibited to tourists in the 1920s. Even parts of the loom mentioned in some versions of the legend were shown.

The basic plot is as follows: One young vallkulla stays at the fäbod to finish work after the others have left in the fall. One night, she is awakened by trolls entering her cabin and making the arrangements for a wedding. One of the trolls is a bridegroom. The trolls dress the vallkulla as a bride. Her dog, sensing that something is wrong, runs home to the village for help. Her fiance rides up just in time and fires a gunshot over the cabin, which makes the trolls disappear and leaves the vallkulla dressed as a bride. She donates the wedding crown to the church, where it is used for years, then lost. (Swedish churches own wedding crowns, which they lend to brides for their weddings. It is a source of great pride for a congregation to own as beautiful and elaborate a crown as possible.)

Different versions adapt to local situations. In some fäbodar that are close to the village, the vallkulla is weaving. But in versions told at far-away fäbodar, she stays behind to let the animals eat the hay collected in the barns. How the message gets to the village varies: the dog runs off on his own; she ties a red string around the dog's neck and sends him home; a voice wakes her father by calling out, "Here you lie, sleeping like a fool, while your daughter is standing as a bride up at the fäbod." In some versions, the father rescues the vallkulla; in others, it is her fiance. They rescue her by shooting over the cabin, throwing an axe over it or over the girl, or by calling out to her to make the sign of the Holy Cross. All versions give detailed descriptions of the beauty of the wedding dress and the abundance of jewelry. The vallkulla gets to keep something of the bridal jewelry, most often the wedding crown, which is usually donated to the local church. In most cases, the crown is mysteriously lost: "It was probably melted down during a famine" or "Nobody knows where it is now." Vänjan and Äppelbo churches, however, still have theirs. In the latter, the troll crown was so big that they made three crowns from it. One they gave to Naas, one to Järna, but they lost theirs.

When a legend becomes as popular as this one did inside the

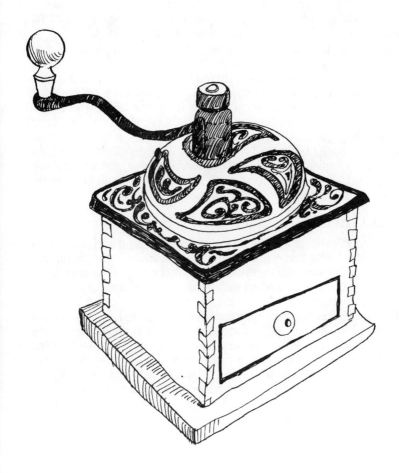

fäbod area, it must have struck a resonant core of response. Among the elements that would be attractive to vallkullor are the themes of loneliness, the threat from trolls that look and act a lot like people, the fear of being kidnapped, especially at a time like the eve of the wedding, the psychological comfort of rescue from the village, as if the story were telling the girl that the extended family really did care, the desire for a beautiful wedding dress and rich jewelry, which the vallkulla can use to "repay" the village by donation to the church. The naming of the church brings the story home and makes it more believable.

Carl von Sydow explores the possible origins of this story. A tired vallkulla, lonely, missing her fiancée, and looking forward to her upcoming wedding, might have drifted off to sleep and had a dream just like the story, for the elements would be the ones on her mind. Her fiance might have been on his way up to the fäbod and fired a shot to signal that he was on the way. The shot awakened the vallkulla; the wedding guests disappeared so quickly they must have been trolls. This story became a living art form that definitely titilates the audience's imagination, and thus it spread over the area where it was understood at once. The fäbod area's border to the south became the border for the distribution of the legend."

4. LEGENDS ABOUT GIANTS

In Swedish tales, giants are a race removed in time and place from the humans. In the fäbod area, to the vallkulla living in the mountains, they were more like neighbors or former inhabitants of the area. In no tales, however, do they interact with people at the fäbod, for the giants belong to another age.

The fäbod area between Mockfjärd and Grangärde has an unusually rich giant lore. It is an area of steep cliffs, giant boulders, and unexplained mounds of stones. Several legends about three giants, Alten, Basten, and Tansen, come from this area. Most of the legends relate how the giants built a road, or dug a lake, or they point out cliffs or caves where these giants once lived, or explain features of the landscape. A growth of Daphne bushes along a ridge, for example, is explained as having been planted there by Alten to keep out Basten and Tansen because he once got mad at them.

Most of the legends are about Basten, who once lived where Bastberget's fäbodar now stands. At one spot on the north side of the fäbod settlement, the ground gives back a hollow sound when people walk on it. Basten hoarded his wealth in a basement there. At another place is a mound of fine sand. Basten was carrying a sack of sand to build a road, but the sack broke and all the sand leaked out.

At Bastberget's fäbodar, there are some ruins of an earlier settlement—fences built of layers upon layers of stones so huge that they impress everyone. The legend is that no man could have done that much work, so it must have been Basten's accomplishment.

These stone fences around the ancient fields and the scattered stone mounds might belong to a Viking age settlement, or even earlier settlers. The area could have been the stronghold of a clan chief, or 'Big Man,' who had to move his family and slaves off into the forest for political reasons. Legends about 'Grey Farmer' exist in the area, parallel to the legends about Basten. Grey Farmer was a mighty man who lived out in the forest with his slaves, broke the ground, and intimidated the valley people. Daniel Brandt speculates that a clan chief from the south, needing to escape Ingjard Illrådes murder plots around 800 A.D., could have found a sanctuary in the Bastberg area. When the settlement was abandoned for reasons unknown, the memory of this man stayed on and legends grew up around him, which later were transposed into legends about the giant Basten.

5. LEGENDS ABOUT LOST COWS

In an area where losing cows was a common reality, it is no surprise that there are many legends about lost cows. Typical is this tale which Marit-Järke's father told to Fräs Erik Andersson:

"I got a message from the fäbod that a cow was lost. I walked eastward and searched there two or three days, but I sure didn't see no cow. And it wasn't easy for one man alone to find a lost cow in these forests that extend for miles and miles, and besides, Randa might have just taken her.

"When I started to suspect that things might have gone wrong with the cow, I started thinking about going to 'Johanna-at-the-Mill' to get help. Johanna could get lost things back. And she wasn't expensive.

"When I got to the mill—its name was Svabensverk, but it was called just the mill—there was a lot of people there ahead of me, just as it usually was at Johanna's. She saw us one by one, in the order we had arrived, and she never made a mistake on that either.

"When my turn came, Johanna came out on her porch and said, 'Well, come on in, and I'll soon tell you what's the matter with your cow. You walked so close to her that you could have taken hold of her tail.'

"When we got to her consulting room—it was the parlor behind the kitchen—she said, 'Sit down now and tell me how your farm is built, and I'll see if I can help you get your cow back.'

"I told her some things I thought would be of use to her, but I left out some small details that I thought were of no consequence. But Johanna got almost angry and said, 'If you don't want to tell me the truth, I'll tell it for you. For example, your brother, Sammil, has a barn behind your house.'

"She said this to let me know that she knew a lot, so one couldn't fib to her in any way. For it was true that Sammil, my brother, had a small barn behind the farmhouse, but I had thought it was too unimportant to mention.

"She started over again. 'You see, it's like this. Randa has your cow. But if you follow my advice, you'll free her from Randa's grip and you'll get your cow back tomorrow afternoon. The cow will then be coming along the northeast road, the Malmsberg trail as you call it, and she'll be wild from fear, as if she had gone mad. You must close the gate to the southwest road, the Flytås trail, for she wants to run in there, and if she does, you can't catch her until you've been back to me one more time. When you catch her, lock her in the barn, pet her, and talk nicely to her, and care for her well, and don't let her out until she is herself again.'

"I walked all the way back up to the fäbod and did exactly as Johanna had said. And, can you imagine! The cow returned exactly as she had said it would. The vallkullor and I had a difficult time with her, for she acted like she had gone crazy. Almost a week passed before she was herself again.

"Now, there's a lot of people that have asked and asked what acts Johanna told me to perform at the fäbod to get the cow back. But I thought they asked only out of curiosity, and if I told them, they would just laugh at me and call me a fool, so I made up my mind not to tell no one. And I've kept that promise. They can wait till they lose something, and then they'll see how funny it is."

This story about a lost cow is one among many which point out the commercial value of cows by reporting in detail the long and intricate search.

6. LEGENDS ABOUT LOST CHILDREN

Many vallkullor brought their young children with them to the fäbod for the summer. The deeper into the forest the fäbod lay, the greater the danger of getting lost. This was particularly true for children. No wonder, then, that the tales about children disappearing were told with a special tone of sympathy and fear.

The following legend comes from Mora:

Near the end of the 18th century, a tragedy happened at Hållindans fäbod. A vallkulla and her three-year-old son walked out into the forest to strip leaves. She put the child on a fallen tree and started to strip leaves nearby. She heard the boy call, "Mama, where are you?" and she walked back to the tree where she had left her son. He was gone!

She ran looking for him and calling his name for as long as she could, but didn't find him. She ran back to the fäbod and told what had happened. Every vallkulla went out searching all night. The following day, a message was sent to the village to tell people to organize a search party. They came from both Vinås and Vika. For two days, they searched without success.

The poor vallkulla, Per's Anna, my grandfather's sister, did not hold up under the heavy sorrow. She became feeble-minded. On a Sunday, her sufferings ended—she fell down dead, next to the grindstone she was turning.

Late that fall, a hunter come walking near Hållindans fäbod. He found there a child's shoe and parts of a shirt. He brought these to the village and showed them to Base Anders, the boy's father, and he recognized them. But who had kidnapped the child was never found out. During those years, there were a lot of bears and wolves in the forest.

Physical evidence suggests that often these legends about lost children were based on facts. For example, an inscription carved in a log above a cabin door at Molbackens fäbod reads: "1718 on Midsummer Day disappeared a daughter Anna age 6."

7. GHOST STORIES TOLD AT THE FÄBOD

Two kinds of ghost stories were told at the fäbod. One was connected with deaths in and around the village; the other with the ghosts of murdered babies.

The first kind of ghost story was told for the pleasure of scaring listeners. This sort usually had little to do with the fäbod itself, but the ghosts of people who had committed suicide or met an awful death through accident. These ghosts often threatened people. For example:

A woman was walking home late one night, pulling a sled. She had been warned against walking too close to the leaning pine tree where Larsgårds Hans had frozen to death. She got too close to the tree and her sled tipped over three times. Only after she had pronounced Jesus's name could she continue.

More closely connected to the vallkullor's life at the fäbod were the ghost stories of murdered infants, as discussed in the previous chapter. How often these murders took place is impossible to know. In Dalarna, strong social pressure was exerted on a man to marry a girl he had made pregnant. But if he was already married, or simply denied he was involved, the situation for the young woman became quite difficult. Legend has it that some pregnant young vallkullor resorted to drastic measures. Most frequently in these legends, the murdered babies are buried under cabin floors or near creeks.

8. LEGENDS ABOUT EPIDEMICS

Legends about epidemics held an awesome place in the folklore of the fäbod area. Many of these legends go back to the devastating effects of the Black Death in the mid-14th century. Even as late as 1710-11, about fifteen percent of Sweden's population died from the Black Death. Epidemics of cholera, typhoid, and influenza were an ever-present threat and kept these horror stories alive.

The "Mali Bambo" legend illustrates this group. Up at Rosberg's fäbod, west of Sollerön, there is a large boulder called Mali Bambo. "IE5E" is chiseled on its side; the "E's" are backward "3's"—that is, the date represented is 1353, the year the Black Death epidemic reached it peak. Beside the boulder and fastened to a tree trunk stands a tall, old grandfather clock from Mora. Everyone who walks by there winds the clock up in memory of the dead.

> During the days the Black Death was spreading throughout our area, a man with a broom and a woman with a rake were seen walking around. They dropped food and jewelry on the ground. If one fell for the temptation and picked up the food or jewelry, one soon broke out with dark spots all over the body. That was a sign that one had become the prey of the Black Death and, before the next sunset, would be dead. If one saw a woman raking in front of a house at twilight, one knew that one person in that house would die, but if the man were also there, sweeping with his broom, everyone would die. People moved toward Norway, out of fear of the Black Death, not knowing that it was just as bad there, if not worse.
>
> Among those that decided to move was Malin, a young woman known for her beauty and virtue, and her girlfriend, whose name is forgotten.
>
> When the girls got a bit beyond Rossberg's fäbodar, Malin saw a golden cross lying in the path. It reminded her of Jesus's sufferings and, forgetful of everything else, she pressed the cross to her lips. She stopped at the big boulder next to the spot where she found the cross and prayed. But when the evening sun hid in the west, her soul flew with the last of the sun's rays to a better place and her lifeless body fell down on the boulder.
>
> When the villagers heard of her death, the minister and some parishioners walked up. They sang mass for Malin and buried her under the rock, while the church bells rang.

Well into this century, vallkullor decorated the Mali Bambo rock at Midsummer with flowers and green leaves. The men took off their hats and prayed when they walked by the boulder. They wound up the big clock, standing nearby.

Further west, there is another ending to the legend of Mali Bambo. Malin is said to have stayed at the fäbod, helping the sick who had gathered there. These sick people walked every day to the boulder and prayed. When Malin became ill and died, she was buried under the boulder.

9. LEGENDS ABOUT WOLVES AND BEARS

As long as beasts lurked around the fäbod, stories about wolves and bears must have expressed the fear and anxiety of the vallkullor. In later days, these same legends were told to express great admiration for the inventive and brave vallkullor.

A bear had grabbed a goat and was pulling it away. The vallkulla grabbed the other end of the goat and pulled, screaming, "Is it your goat, or is it mine?" The bear had to give up and wander off.

In Malung, a story was told of a vallkulla who saw a bear among her cows. "She got so mad at him that she hit him with the drop-spindle she was working with. The bear got angry and hit her back, taking a large part of her scalp. She managed to survive."

Other legends tell how some vallkullor barked like dogs to scare off a bear, or threw a burning branch so that the bear's pelt caught on fire, or scared him off with loud noise. "One vallkulla was very brave. A bear had come too close to her cows, and she took her small axe and whacked it into his backbone. The next summer, they found the bear lying dead, with the axe still in his back."

Some of these legends are tragic, telling about vallkullor who didn't survive their encounters with bears or wolves, while others can be rather humorous.

Lekatt Mats' grandpa told of a bear that had killed a cow near Kilen's fäbod. Each evening, the bear came back to eat more of the cow. Some old men decided to kill the bear. They filled a big pot with aquavit (a strong liquor, much like vodka) and half-buried the pot next to the dead cow. Then they hid in the bushes. The bear came, sniffed the liquor, snorted, and drank it all up.

After a while, the bear sat down on his hind legs, waved his arms about, and roared. Then he sank down, asleep, snoring loudly. The men crept forward and killed him.

There are far fewer legends about wolves, perhaps because they are shy and attack more slyly than bears. One vallkulla who was bothered by wolves sneaking around the corners of her cabin did what she could with the circumstances: she burned an old shoe in her fireplace. The smell was so awful, the wolves left.

There seem to be no legends about combat with wolves. They were mostly scared off by loud sounds blown on the lur or horn.

151

THE LEGENDS PERSIST

Many of these legends have themes that are familiar all over the world, but they persist in Dalarna (much as they persist in other places) as local history in local costume, as the experience of local people. This persistence was fed by the telling and retelling of the stories as the truth. Sometimes, this truth was attested to by the most respectable members of the culture. One of the most interesting of these testimonials was written down by a minister, Petrus Rahm, in the 17th century.

The minister and his wife were at their fäbod one evening, when a small man came in, asking for help. The small man's wife was in labor and he needed help from the minister's wife. Petrus Rahm describes the man's clothing and how he and his wife hesitated, but at last they agreed. Out of fear of revenge, Petrus Rahm told his wife to go, and he recited prayers for her.

When she came back to the fäbod cabin at 10 p.m., she told her husband that she had been brought through the air to a front door, which they entered. The minister's wife helped with the birth of the child. She was then offered some food, but refused it and returned to her cabin.

> The following morning, (writes Rahm) my wife found a set of silver spoons on a shelf in the cabin, and we understood that the vittra-people had put them there. That this really happened exactly as I wrote it down, I hereby sign my name to
>
> Ragunda April 12, 1671 Petrus Rahm

With such testimony, many a vallkulla could convince herself she wasn't fibbing when she told her tales about forest beings!

CHAPTER FOURTEEN

COURTING AND FESTIVE ACTIVITIES

Although the vallkullor were separated from their villages and isolated in the mountains, they did manage to have a social life. In many ways, this social life reconstructed the life of the village; women continued to socialize in domestic ways, boys came courting, groups gathered for games and dancing. In other ways, however, society paid special attention to the vallkulla, especially at the time of her homecoming.

The most common kind of socializing, of course, was among the women at the fäbod. In spite of a heavy work load, they found time to visit each other's cabins in the evenings. Some evenings, for example, they would arrange a knitting competition. They would gather in one cabin, start a fire in the fireplace, and hold a contest. They would measure up equal lengths of yarn for each participant; at a given signal, they would all start knitting; the winner was the one who used up her thread quickest.

They also tried to arrange their work so that they had as much time as possible free on Sundays, so that they could get together, often outdoors and enjoy visiting, singing, and drinking coffee. As Hilda Liljas explained, "There were many of us young women at Ertled fäbod . . . we went to each other and talked and played games in the yard. Sundays, we dressed a little better (we never herded on Sundays), but elegant dresses like today's we didn't have."

The vallkullor played many practical jokes on each other. Some told that they dressed up in men's clothes and went snooping around in the dusk, courting at other fäbodar. One favorite trick was to fill a pair of men's pants with grass and place   them in the outdoor toilet, along with a pair of old shoes, and leave the door ajar, showing the "man's" legs. Or they placed a "grass stuffed man" in some conspicuous place; then, in the dusk or evening, they would ask the others, "Who is that sitting out there in the dark?"

Saturday evenings, many young men walked the trails up to the fäbodar, mostly in groups. The distance to the fäbod or the serious-ness of the love affair determined how many visitors came. One women explained "we hoped visitors would come, so we decorated the cabins with wild flowers and green branches, put on a clean dress, and cooked something good to eat. We never knew who would be coming. Often the boys from Bjurs village came, but it was more fun when the boys from Börn and Gärdesbyn came, for they brought fiddlers."

At one fäbod, the vallkullor organized these Saturday night visits to some extent. At a certain spot that everyone was familiar with, they would place, right side up, as many spruce twigs as there were unmarried girls at the fäbod. Each boy who walked up to that fäbod turned one spruce twig wrong side up. When all twigs were turned over, it was a message to the rest of the boys that all the girls were "taken" and they had better walk on to another fäbod.

On the first visit to the fäbod for the summer, the boys were not sure who was there, and they could be shy. Ann Ericsson-Hayton explained:

"As soon as the boys got within sight of the cabin, they stopped singing. In a way, they were shy and didn't want to make too much noise. They were not sure who was at the fäbod, and they were afraid that there might be some old strict vallkulla among us. Usually, some of us girls went out and invited them in. Then we danced in the cabin that had the most even floor. In the beginning, the boys didn't dare to invite the girls to dance, so we danced with each other, and then the boys slowly joined us. The younger boys, the ones fifteen or sixteen years old, played games outside, wrestled, and peeked in the windows, before they dared to come inside. When we finished dancing, the boys slept in the hay-lofts or outdoors."

The weeks when the grass on the bogs and meadows was cut was a high light of the summer, a really funfilled time for the vallkullor and their visitors. Knis Karl remembers that the vallkullor decorated the biggest hay-loft at Bastberg's fäbod with birch saplings those weeks. A lot of people were there then. There was rhythmical stomping at Jacob's hay-loft to the tunes from accordian and fiddle. Waltzes and polkas were danced the most. Sometimes, dance-games were played in Backolle's flat front yard. These dances were held until about 1920.

Adults and young children, as well as the vallkullor, joined in the dance-games. A particular set of movements, which everyone soon learned, belonged to each melody sung and played in a dance-game. One dance-game, for example, began with the participants in two big circles, women in one, men in the other. As the song and game progressed, the circles moved, broke up, formed smaller groups and pairs who skipped and danced in place. At the end of the song, everyone formed a single big circle.

These haying weeks were filled, not only with dances, but also games, riddles, jokes, story-telling, and an abundance of practical jokes played on the opposite sex. Many remember that those light summer nights at the fäbodar were filled with laughter, and quite a few looked back on them in years afterwards as their fondest memories.

COURTSHIP

While the fäbod isolated the girls from their villages for a good part of the summer, it also introduced greater mobility, especially social mobility, into their lives. During the winters, the young people didn't meet many people from outside their village. But, at the fäbod, the girls worked with or visited women and girls from several villages and met men from other villages when they were visiting the fäbod. Many marriages were the result of a fäbod summer.

In the villages, there existed a traditional custom called "night courting," which followed set rules. Many girls moved out of the main house when they reached the courting age and lived in one of the other buildings on the farm. There, young people met evenings and sang, danced, and played games. When a couple started taking a liking to each other, the young man was allowed to stay overnight, at first sleeping on top of the blanket with only his shoes removed.

This custom was also accepted at the fäbod. One way a girl could let a boy know that it was all right with her if he stayed all night was by secretly slipping him a "pearl" of chewing pitch from a spruce tree.

Midsummer has always meant a big, happy celebration in Sweden. A maypole decorated with leaves and flowers is erected in each village, good foods are prepared and eaten, and dances are held outdoors and last way into the night. At the fäbod, the vallkullor did what they could to imitate the village celebration. Even those vallkullor living so far out in the forest that they received no visitors tried to celebrate Midsummer by decorating with wildflowers and cooking special festive dishes they enjoyed.

HOMEWARD BOUND

If the move up to the fäbod in the spring generated happiness and excitement, so did the move home in the fall, particularly in those vallkullor who lived very far out in the forests. Custom throughout the fäbod area made this homecoming a major social event.

During the last week at the fäbod, the vallkullor were allowed, by an age-old tradition, to use the milk for themselves. They made very small cheeses of fresh whole milk in special molds. These were called "little cheese" and they were not much larger than a deck of cards. These "little cheeses" played an important part in the homecoming social activities.

A day or two before the move home, people from the farm walked up to the fäbod to help close the buildings for the winter and help carry the milk products home.

"The last night, we didn't get much sleep. Every vessel and utensil had to be scrubbed clean and stored in the milk-house; the cast iron pots had to be rubbed with unsalted butter, so they wouldn't rust; every vent had to be stuffed full of grass or mosses, so no snow would blow in; the bedding had to be hung over a pole near the ceiling; the cabin had to be scrubbed, floors, table, stools, benches, shelves; everything had to be clean. The hay used for bedding was poured into the barn, and the backpacks had to be carefully loaded with the cheeses, whey butter and butter."

In spite of the work, this was a time of great merry making. In 1881, Arborelius wrote this description of the move home:

"The vallkullor stayed up all through the last night, because they had so much work to do. A lot of joking went on. The hike home was very jovial, too. As many vallkullor as possible walked together, all dressed in the best clothes they could manage. They sang melodies in the kulning technique and were not stingy with handing out flour and salt to the cows. When the cows realized that they were leaving the grazing trails and turning into the homeward bound trails, they too took part in the general jovial mood, jumping and running, bellowing as if they were wild."

One of the best descriptions of how the villages saw this move home from the fäbod was told to Knis Karl in 1960 by Mor Anders Ersson (born 1868):

"You look at TV and see pictures from New York and China and all that, but I have seen something that nobody will see any more, and it was exceptional. At Djura lake, several fäbod teams met up to let the animals drink. Hundreds of cows, goats, and packhorses came out of the forests sloping down to the lake. The bells rang, the vallkullor sang kulning and blew in their horns, and there was laughter all over, a celebration without comparison. But you don't get to see that, even if you see pictures from all over the world."

The bell cow was singled out for special treatment when she walked home. In Leksand, she was called "the bride" for that day. And around her neck, the vallkulla hung a very special chain, which was decorated with small squares of bright, colorful cloth. The other cows often wore around their necks all the chains and withes the vallkulla had made during the summer.

HOMECOMING CELEBRATIONS

The move home was most often done on a Saturday, so that celebrations could take place Saturday evening and Sunday. The vallkullor walked the cows to the farm they belonged to and handed them over. The farmer's wife had a big dinner ready and the vallkulla was the center of attention. The milk products were then admired and the cows and goats checked over, and all the knitted and sewn items given to the household. These hours were very special for the employed vallkulla and crucial to her relationship with her employers. She got the chance to show the quality of her work, display her skills and industriousness. If the farmer and his wife were pleased with her work, they told her so and often would invite her to work for them again the following summer. For the vallkulla who belonged to the extended family, it must have been a great pleasure to come home and see the cellar filled for the winter with the milk products she had produced.

Both the employed vallkulla and the one belonging to the family had made several of the "little cheeses." The married ones gave theirs to the family, to the children in particular.

For the unmarried vallkullor, these "little cheeses" carried a lot more implications—and complications! Local custom varies a great deal, but a common denominator seems to have been the practice of the young men of the village confronting the vallkulla and demanding a taste of her cheeses that first evening home from the fäbod. If a vallkulla was engaged, she would have made a very special "little cheese," showing all the skill and artistry she had; this "little cheese" she gave to her fiance. He could judge what kind of house-wife she would be from the quality of the cheese. If a girl was secretly fond of a boy, she could get that message across by giving him a whole cheese. All others would get just a slice or two. In some areas, the boys were given slices at a dance held that first night home. In other areas, no dance was held, but a regular "give-me-cheese-chase" took place. The girls hid, and the boys searched for the girls with a lot of hustling and laughter. When a boy found a girl, he demanded a taste of the "little cheese." In some villages, this turned out to be an all-involved bit of merrymaking: the farmer himself helped hide his vallkulla and refused to tell the boys where she was. It could be heard all over the village, they say, when a vallkulla was found.

It was important that the vallkulla had made enough of these "little cheeses," or else she would be in trouble, as is recorded from Boda:

If the boys all got a slice of cheese, everything was all right, but, if they didn't, trouble was ahead for the vallkulla. The boys would locate a cart and borrow it. The girl would be pulled, screaming from the house—even out of bed in her night gown—and placed in the cart. The boys would run, pulling the cart way off, preferably downhill. When they decided they had gotten far enough, they would tip the girl out, leaving her to walk home alone, pulling the cart. No wonder the girls saw to it that they had enough cheese to go around.

The next day, Sunday, the vallkullor were the center of the village's attention. The farmer that had employed her gave her a ride to church. Custom required that he should drive his horses so fast that the vallkulla's kerchief tied around her head should billow out behind her. The faster the speed, the greater the honor.

Custom also called for a special dress that first Sunday. When the people of Dalarna went to church, everyone wore his or her local costume, which varies a great deal in color and design from county to county. The color of the woman's apron and the bodice changed according to set rules with the church year. The normal costume for Leksand women was a red and white striped apron and a simple red bodice. But a blue apron, a more elaborate red bodice, and a richly embroidered scarf were worn on most festive occasions, Christmas, New Year's Day, Easter Sunday, Whit Sunday, Midsummer Day, and at weddings. The vallkullor wore this outfit when they went to church that first day home from the fäbod. They were dressed as brides, so that everybody could see who had been brave enough to be a vallkulla. They were greatly admired and honored in the churchyard when the services were over.

In most areas, another dance was held on Sunday evenings to honor the vallkullor. The young men saw to it that no vallkulla sat out a dance, but had a grand time.

CHAPTER FIFTEEN

THE FÄBOD TODAY

During the last decades of the 19th century, the use of the fäbodar was at a maximum. Each available straw of grass in the forest and on the bogs was used. Then followed a long period of decline. No definite date can be set for when this happened, nor can one find any reliable statistics about it. Montelius mentions that the decline in Leksand county spans almost a hundred years. In other counties, the process went much faster. Several economic conditions influenced the process of decline, though these conditions varied from area to area. Psychological factors were also involved in how late or how early a fäbod was abandoned.

During the last decades of the 19th century, a farm organization began to teach modern techniques to farmers in Dalarna, such as the use of fertilizers, the use of new and improved tools, and the planting of improved strains of grain. Some farmers were quicker than others to adopt the new ideas and methods, which resulted in great crop variations in a relatively small area.

The new techniques brought a higher yield of grain per acre. This, in turn, freed some farm land for the growing of hay. The farmers soon found out that they could grow more hay on the fields near the village with considerably less work than cutting and gathering it way out in the forest.

The areas in the forest that yielded the least amount of hay were abandoned earliest. The others followed successively, in some areas rapidly, in some areas more slowly. Some forest areas were still in use during World War II. Perhaps Walter Michelsson was the last farmer to cut grass on a bog in Dalarna. He did it, not by hand, but with a tractor, as late as mid-1960.

At the same time as hay began to be cultivated in the fields near the villages, local dairies began to appear. In some areas, dairies were built as early as the beginning of the century; in others, it was thirty to forty years later. The dairies, of course, did not look favorably upon the cows being gone all summer, and they urged the abandonment of the fäbod system, so that they would be assured milk deliveries even in the summer. This resulted in one farmer after the next keeping his cows home all year.

Other farmers, in areas where no dairy was built yet, began a partial abandonment of the fäbod system too. They kept a couple of cows on the farm during the summer to keep the family in fresh milk. When, some year, they had difficulty finding a vallkulla, it was not such a big step to keep all the cows at home.

Emotional, psychological, and traditional elements played a role in counteracting the economic reasons for abandoning the fäbod system and slowed the process. One often hears comments like, "It didn't feel like summer if we didn't get to go up to the fäbod," and "We kept the fäbod going as long as Mother lived." Verna Smids at Lindorna fäbod answered my question with, "Oh, I come up here, partly because we can use the farm fields for cash crops better, but mostly because I like it. It's so quiet and peaceful up here at our fäbod. And our kids really enjoy themselves here." Gerda Träff at Årteråsens fäbod answered with, "It's my vacation to come up here every summer. Besides that, I get to meet so many wonderful people, the tourists, that walk up to see the fäbod and learn about it."

In some areas the idea of abandoning the fäbod swept almost like a fad. "If Olssons did it, and Anderssons too, then we'll stay at home next summer also."

It is ironic that the period of decline began at about the same time as there was an increase in the available grazing areas in the forest. Bogs and meadows that had been saved for haying were successively opened up for grazing. Logging increased at that time, which meant that large areas were cleared by the loggers. Grass grew on these areas in abundance.

It is also ironic that the decline period coincided with a marked improvement in the roads to and from the fäbodar. The loggers built bigger and better roads, deeper and deeper into the forests, to get the logs out efficiently. It became easier and easier to drive closer and closer to the fäbod, just at the time the farmers no longer wanted to get there.

After a long period of disuse, the fäbodar are being used again today, but their function has changed considerably.

Many of the empty fäbod buildings have disappeared. Some of them were sold for firewood during World War II, when Sweden couldn't import enough coal for heating homes. But the greatest cause of disappearance was rot. The buildings would hold up as long as the roof held, but once the roof had rotted, it didn't take long for the walls to crumble also. This was the fate of most of the fäbodar that were farthest out in the forest. The hay barns are almost all gone now; so are many of the animal barns. The cabins that survived through the 1940s, and they total a large number, are now treasured and lovingly cared for—as the vacation homes of the grandchildren of vallkullor.

During the 1920s, several fäbodar near Leksand sold to rich or upper class people from Stockholm and were converted to second homes to be used during the summer. Some of the attempts to modernize the buildings went overboard and local humor baptized the area, "The Millionaires' Summer Camp." Since the 1950s, it has been virtually impossible for an outsider to buy a fäbod, or an empty lot in a fäbod settlement. Many of the farmers would never think of selling their fäbodar; instead they keep them, enjoying picnics there, or their children and grandchildren spend some weeks there during the summer and winter vacations.

Some tourist organizations bought up some sixty fäbodar in the 1950s and began renting them out as vacation cabins. Dalarna is one of the more popular tourist areas, and a lot of people spend their summers in the forests and mountains there.

During the early years of transforming the fäbodar into vacation homes, some tasteless remodelings were done. To put a porch with a green corrugated roof on a fäbod cabin is really too much of a break in style.The Swedes have become increasingly aware of the cultural value of the old buildings and strong interests have centered on preserving them. If any remodeling or additions are to be done, they must be absolutely authentic to the style of the building. For example, if a new roof is needed on a fäbod cabin, the local building code permits the use of tar-paper to keep the water out, but birch bark should be used along the edges where it is visible.

Several cultural-historical organizations got together under the direction of Skansen, Sweden's largest outdoor museum, and Nordiska Museet, the largest national museum, and published a book, **"Skansens handbok i vården av gamla byggnader"** (Skansen's Handbook for the Care of Old Buildings) in 1953. From that date on, an increasing number of committees have been formed nationally, as well as locally, to assist and guide the owners of old buildings, from log cabin to castle, in the task of preserving them.

The old fäbod teams met to agree on the date for the repair of fences, the move to the fäbod, and the like, Today's fäbod teams meet regularly to dicuss such issues as the upkeep of roads and fences, sanitary questions, construction of parking lots outside the fäbod settlement, future expansions and their desirability. If one member wants to add or remodel, his plans have to be studied and permission given. Since trees invade the meadows, they have to be cut at least every two years; the fäbod team sets the date for that work, in which all members must participate.

In the last few years, many fäbod teams have built new fences around the meadows and kept sheep at the fäbod to eat any tree saplings before they destroy the meadows. Many of the fäbodar have lost their feeling of openness and their beautiful views of the valleys because the forest has grown upon the meadows that once surrounded the fäbod. From the minutes of a Forsbodarna fäbod team's meeting comes this interesting note: "It was suggested that another rule be added: the ones who want to keep cows at the fäbod should be allowed to do so, and the neighbors may not complain about animals walking around."

On August 6, 1980, this item appeared in a newspaper, Falu-Kuriren:

Many persons are waiting for building permits to build cabins at Västtjärnslindans fäbodar in Gagnef. All own land there already, but the county commission would not grant permits until they had met with the fäbod team and discussed the question. . . It was agreed that the shape and structure of the old fäbod settlement must be maintained. New buildings should be located outside the present area. The new buildings must look like the old cabins, and the team wanted control of that . . . Warnings were issued. If too many new buildings were permitted, the new owners might make demands for water, sewer, and electricity. They must accept the fäbod as it is—without modern conveniences, which would destroy the old fäbod. 'Gärdesgårdar (the old fences) and electrical lines don't mix,' said Sigfried Andersson.

The fäbodar in Dalarna today are very much a part of the social life. The local ski clubs arrange several cross-country ski trips, using the fäbodar as rest stops. In the summers, they and other clubs arrange hikes between fäbodar. All the counties surrounding Lake Siljan have cooperated in building and mapping out a trail called "**Siljansleden**" which follows the old fäbod trail to a large extent. Copies of the old haying sheds have been built for overnight sleeping. Most of the local crafts guilds, home-preservation clubs, and museums arrange picnics with music and lectures at fäbodar each summer. Folkmusic festivals are held at fäbodar, as well as week-long courses in which the old fäbod life is relived.

All through the summer, the different fäbodar take turns arranging for church services to be held at the fäbod. It is popular to have weddings and baptisms and other church events at the fäbod. One minister sighed and commented that he got more persons to come to the fäbod service than to church.

The fäbodar that still operate in the old way have also changed. Some of their income comes from selling cheeses, butter, and whey butter to the tourists, but the main part comes from selling coffee. The coffee pot thus still stands hot all day, if not in the open fireplace, at least on the kitchen stove.

To many villagers and visitors, the fäbod is an emotional tie with times passed. Montelius remarks that many old people have told him that

> "...there, in a beautiful way, one comes in almost personal contact with one's ancestors who walked the cattle lanes and trails for hundreds of years; there one can sit inside the same cabin as earlier generations and one can sit by the same open hearth as great-great grandma and, in the light of the dying embers, seek answers to many questions."

When an old man in Leksand was asked what he thought it would be like to die, he answered, "Well, I guess it'll be like going to some far-away fäbod."

REFERENCES

A. PERSONAL INTERVIEWS

1. Blomkvist, Anna (b. 1902). Gagnef, Sweden. 15 July 1980.
2. Blomkvist, Kerstin (b. 1904). Gagnef, Sweden. 15 July 1980.
3. Blomkvist, Thilda (b. 1908). Gagnef, Sweden. 15 July 1980.
4. Bäckström, Anna (b. 1923). Gagnef, Sweden. 17 July 1980.
5. Hane, Anders (b. 1909). Gagnef, Sweden. 25 July 1980.
6. Hane, Ida (b. 1909). Gagnef, Sweden. 30 June, 22-25 July 1980.
7. Jakobsson, Pelle (b. 1923). Orsa, Sweden. 9, 17 July 1980.
8. Jobs-Björklöv, Kersti (b. 1937). Leksand, Sweden. 15 July 1980.
9. Liss, Anna (b. 1899). Gagnef, Sweden. 7 Jan 1976.
10. Liss, Hjalmar (b. 1922). Leksand, Sweden. 17 July 1980.
11. Niss, Edit (b. 1911). Gagnef, Sweden. 30 June 1980.
12. Smids, Verna (b. 1931). Orsa, Sweden. 3 July 1980.
13. Sterner-Jonsson, Lilley (b. 1900). Sollern, Sweden. 2 July 1980.
14. Träff, Gerda (b. 1926). Furudal, Sweden. 5 July 1980.

B. UNPUBLISHED MANUSCRIPTS

15. Aronsson, Knis Karl. "Upteckningar om fäbodar i Leksand och Siljansnäs."Leksands Kommunalkontor (Office of the County Commissioner), undated.
16. Björklund, Ulla. "Vallhjon och vallning." University of Uppsala, Sweden, 1966.
17. Boethius, Lena. "fäbodar i Gagnef och Mockfjärd." University of Uppsala, Sweden, 1967.
18. Dalmalm, Gustav. "Djura och Skebergsbygden i saga och hävd." Leksands Kommunalkontor, 1966.
19. Helmer, Robert H. P. "European Pastoral Calls and their Possible Influence on Western Liturgical Chant." Diss. Columbia University 1975.
20. Homman, Olle. "Om övernaturliga väsen." Unpublished field notes, kept in the archives at Dalarnas museum, Falun.
21. Johnson, Anna. "Svenska locklatar i nutidstradition. Studie över storform och funktion." University of Uppsala, Sweden, 1972.
22. Lundberg, Gunilla. "Fäbodväsendet under 1800-talet i amhusfjärdingen." University of Uppsala, Sweden, 1967.
23. Olson, Snibb Anders. "olksägner och folktro i Gagnef." Dalarnas museum, archive 7431-949.

24. Persson, Birgitta. "Försök till kategori indelning av sägner om spökerier och gengangare i Dalarna." University of Uppsala, Sweden, 1961.
25. Pettersson, Täpp Sven-Olov. "Älgsjöselens fäboddrift under 1900-talet. Malungs socken." University of Uppsala, Sweden, 1971.
26. Segerberg, Ann. "Fäbodar i Rättvik och Boda." University of Uppsala, Sweden, 1967.
27. ULMA, Dialekt och folkminnesarkivet. The institute for Dialect and Folklore Research, Uppsala, Sweden.

C. RECORDINGS

28. Ancient Swedish Pastoral Music. Locklatar och musik pa horn och pipa. Sveriges Radio, RELP 5017. n.d.
29. Aronsson, Knis Karl. "Fäbodliv." Lecture at Skinnarasens fäbod, July 8, 1975. Tape recording at Leksand Library.
30. Johnson, Anna. "Sången i skogen, skogen i sången—om fäbod-arnas musik." Swedish Radio broadcast, December 6, 1980.
31. Ramsby, Walter. Latar pa klarinett, spilåpipa, kohorn och lur, spelade i ursprunglig miljö. Sonet, SLP 2043. 1973.

D. PERIODICALS

32. Arborelius, Olof Per. "n fäbodvandring i Vesterdalarna." Ny Illustrerad Tidning, No. 4 (1881), p. 31; No. 5 (1881), pp. 39-42.
33. B. L. "Sägen fran Ljusbodarna." Gammalt och nytt fran Dalarne, (1926 yearbook), p. 126.
34. Bengtsson, Ingvar. "On Melody Registration and 'MONA,'" in Elektronische Datenverarbeitung in der Musikwissenschaft. Regensburg: n.p., 1967.
35. Boethius, Gerda. "Fäbodar och fäbodliv." Dalarnas hembygdsbok, (1943 yearbook), pp. 53-62.
36. Brandt, Daniel. "Sägner om Basten, Alten, och Tansen." Dalarnas hembygdsbok, (1938 yearbook), pp. 180-185.
37. Campbell, Ake. "Det onda ögat och besläktade före-ställningar i svensk folktradition." Folkminnen och Folktankar, 20 (1924), 121-129.
38. ———. "Drag ur övre Dalaranas äldre folkliga tankevärld." Ditt Land, 34 (1945), 22-25.
39. Christiansen, Reider. "The Migratory Legends: a Proposed List of the Types with a Systematic Catalogue of the Norwegian Variants."Folklore Fellows Comunications, 175 (1958), 1-216.

40. Dalmalm, Gustav. "Folket i Dalarna offrade i källor och drack sig must i benen." Mora Tidning, Dec. 4, 1974, p. 4.

41. Danielsson, Bertil. "Minnen och intryck." California Veckoblad, Dec. 5., 1980, p. 3.

42. "Det vernaturliga i gamla tiders Dalarna." Gammalt och nytt fran Dalarne, (1929 yearbook), pp. 51-55.

43. Ekstam, Lina. "Smatt och gott fran 'den gamla goda tiden.'" Dalarnas hembygdsförbunds tidskrift, 3 (1923), 120-122.

44. Erixon, Sigurd. "Bebyggelseundersökningar." Fataburen, 15 (1918), 9-31.

45. ————. "Betesvandringar och flyttsystem." Folk-Liv, 20 (1955-56), 39-46.

46. ————. "Hedbodarnas långfäbod i Älvdalen." Dalarnas hembygdsbok, (1941 yearbook), pp. 81-104.

47. Forselius, Soren. "Skälltillverkningen, ett hantverk som försvinner." Hälsingerunor, 34 (1961), 131-134.

48. Forsslund, Karl-Erik. "Nagra vandringssägner (och en vädjan!)." Meddelanden fran Dalarnas hembygdsförbund, (1920 yearbook), pp. 46-51.

49. af Geijerstam, Claes, and Anna Johnson, eds. "Fäbod-musik i förvandling." Svensk tidskrift for musik-forskning, 60, No. 2 (1978), 5-39.

50. Granlund, John. "Trollformler fran Västmanland och Dalarnas bergslag." Västsvenska fornminnen, (1929 yearbook), pp. 82-103.

51. Hallerdt, Björn. Ärteråsen i Ore." Dalarnas hem-bygdsbok, (1957 yearbook), pp. 39-58.

52. Hedman, Hjalmar. "Fäbodväsen." Dalarnas hembygds-förbunds tidskrift, 8 (1928), 11-16.

53. "Hur man levde i Leksand- och Gagnefstrakten pa 1800-talet." Gammalt och nytt fran Dalarne, (1924 yearbook), pp. 142-143.

54. Johansson, Levi. "Lucia och de underjordiska i norr-ländsk folksägen." Fataburen, 3 (1906), 193-201.

55. Larsson, Nils. "Fäboden får växa med förstand." Falu-Kuriren, August 6, 1980, p. 9.

56. Linnman, Johannes. "Några anteckningar om allmogens mjölkhushallning i Dalarna." Fataburen, 11 (1914), 19-35.

57. Lithberg, Nils. "Koskällan." Fataburen, 11 (1914), 1-18.

58. Liungman, Waldemar. "Sägner fran Värmland om skogsrå och bergfolk." Folkminnen och Folktankar, 24 (1928), 113-123.

59. Moberg, Carl-Allan. "Locklåten om den förlorade (och återfunna) kon." Saga och sed, (1959 yearbook), pp. 81-86.

60. ————. "Om vallåtar. En studie i de svenska fäbodarnas musikaliska organization." Svensk tidskrift for musikforskning, 37 (1955), 7-95.

61. ————. "Om vallåtar II: Musikaliska struktur problem." Svensk tidskrift for musikforskning, 41 (1959), 10-57.
62. Montelius, Anders. "Gagnefs åldringar berättar." Gammalt och nytt fran Dalarne, (1923-24 yearbook), pp. 150-152.
63. Ohlson, Ella. "Naturväsen i angermanländsk folktro." Folkminnen och Folktankar, 29 (1933), 70-79.
64. Oldeberg, Andreas. "Vallhorn, herdepipor och lurar. En studie med utgångspunkt från ett värmländskt järnåldersfynd." Värmland förr och nu, 48 (1950), 19-67.
65. Olsson, Arnold. "Husdjuren i tro och sed." Västsvens ka fornminnen, 19 (1929), 104-111.
66. Olsson, Erikhans H. "Fäbodar och fäbodliv i Boda pa 1800-talet." Dalarnas hembygdsbok, (1940 yearbook), pp. 59-66.
67. Pedersen, Britt-Marie. "Studier rörande fäbodbebyggel sen i Kall." Folk Liv, 17 (1953-54), 19-26.
68. Pentikainen, Juha. "The Nordic Dead-Child Tradition." Folklore Fellows Communications, 202 (1968), 1-388.
69. Persson, Anna. "Hur en vallkulla hade det for 70 år sedan." By Sockengille, 7 (1933), 20-23.
70. "Restaureringsarbetet med Hedbodarna har påborjats." Skansenvakten, 28 (1943), 3-7.
71. Roos, Anna Maria. "Fran Gagnef." Ord och bild, 15 (1906), 251-257.
72. Sterner-Jonsson, Lilly. "Mali-Bambo. Funderingar kring en bygdelegend." Västeras stiftsbok, 64 (1970), 75-82.
73. von Sydow, Carl. "Spöktro och vättetro." Folkminnen och Folktankar, 21 (1925), 1-22.
74. ————. "Trollbröllopet i säterstugan." Fryksände förr och nu, 3 (1931), 99-103.
75. ————. "Övernaturliga väsen." Nordisk Kultur/Folketru, 19, (1935), 95-159.
76. Tegengren, Nils. "Offerstenar." Budkaveln, 9 (1922), 25-59.
77. Trotzig, Liv. "Band som saluslöjd." Hemslöjden, 6 (1979), 29-30.
78. Ullberg, Gösta. "Köuklatar fran Klövsjö." Jämten, 19 (1925), 35-49.
79. Westgards, Anders. "Randan i folktron." Gammalt och nytt fran Dalarne, (1928 yearbook), pp. 206-207.
80. Åhmark, Mats. "Drick hälsan Trefaldighetsafton." Gammalt och nytt fran Dalarne, (1955:56 yearbook), pp. 97-99.

E. BOOKS

81. Berg, Gösta and Sigfrid Svensson, eds. Gruddbo pa Sollerön, en bygdeundersökning. Stockholm: Thule, 1938.
82. Bergmark, Matts. Vallört och vitlök. Stockholm: Natur och Kultur, 1962.
83. Bringeus, Nils-Arvid. Arbete och redskap. Lund: CWK Gleerup, 1973.

84. Dahlstedt, Ture. Tro och föreställningar om vitra i övre Norrland. Umea: Dialekt och ortnamnsarkivet, 1976.
85. Dandanell, Birgitta, and Göran Rosander, eds. Dalaskogen. Falun: Dalarnas museum/Nordiska museet, 1977.
86. Dybeck, Richard. Svenska vallvisor och hornlåtar med norska artförändringar. 1846; rpt. Stockholm: Bok och Bild, 1974.
87. Erixon, Sigurd. "Eldhus." In Svenska kulturbilder, Vol. 7. Stockholm: Skoglunds, 1935, pp. 33-52.
88. ————. "Folklig telegrafering." In Svenska kulturbilder. Vol. 4. Stockholm: Skoglunds, 1935, pp. 31-64.
89. Forsell, H. Sverige i 1571. Stockholm: Bonniers, 1872.
90. Forsslund, Karl-Erik. Med Dalälven fran källorna till havet. 3 Vols. Stockholm: Ahlens och Akerlunds, 1918-1939.
91. Fredlund, Jane. Sa levde vi. Uppsala: ICA, 1971.
92. Frödin, John. Siljansomradets fäbodbygd. Lund: privately printed, 1925.
93. ————. "Svenska fäbodar. In Svenska kulturbilder. Vol. 3. Stockholm: Skoglunds, 1935, pp. 79-97.
94. Gadelius, Bror. Tro och övertro i gångna tider. Stockholm: Gebers, 1912.
95. Gagner, Anders. Gammal folktro fran Gagnef i Dalarna. Malmö: Maiander, 1918.
96. Geijer, E.G., and A. Afzelius. Svenska folkvisor. Stockholm: Haggströms, 1880.
97. Granberg, Gunnar. Skogsraet i yngre nordisk folktradition. Uppsala: Gustav Adolfs Akademie för folklivsforskningen, 1935.
98. Heugren, Paul. Husdjuren i nordisk folktro. Örebro: Örebro Dagblad, 1925.
99. Hakansson, Sven-Gunnar. Bygg och lek med timmer. Västerås: ICA, 1972.
100. Johansson, Levi. "De osynlige." In Festskrift till Eric Festin, Jämtländska Studier, ed. Gösta Berg. Östersund: Heimbygdas förlag, 1928, pp. 224-230.
101. Jonth, Margareta. Visor fran Dalarna. Stockholm: Prisma, 1975.
102. Larsson, John, Karin Forsmark, and Ingrid Hjort. Gagnefs-dräkten. Grycksbo: privately printed, 1976.
103. Leksands Hemslöjdsförening. Almanacka för Leksands-dräkten. Stockholm: privately printed, 1978.
104. Levander, Lars. Övre Dalarnas bondekultur under 1800-talets förra hälft. 3 Vols. Stockholm: Jonsson och Winter, 1944-1947.
105. Lidman, Hans, ed. Fäbodar. Kristianstad: LTs förlag, 1963.
106. Lidman, Hans, and Anders Nyman, eds. Fäbodminnen. Kristianstad: LTs förlag, 1965.
107. Lindholm, Erik, and others. Gagnef och Mockfjärd, en hembygdsbok. Falun: privately printed, 1952.

108. Lindow, John. Swedish Legends and Folktales. Berkeley: University of California Press, 1978.
109. Ling, Jan, and others. Folkmusikboken. Stockholm: Prisma, 1980.
110. Ling, Jan. Svensk folkmusik. Stockholm: Prisma, 1974.
111. Montelius, Sigvard. "Dalarnas fäbodar." In Littera-turvägledning fran Dalarnas biblioteksförbund. Pamphlet 15., ed. Olle Wingborg. Grysckbo: privately printed, 1970.
112. ————. "Fäbodarnas betydelse for näringsliv och bebyggelse. In Gammal bygd blir ny. ed. Stig Björklund. Uppsala: privately printed, 1978, pp. 69-108.
113. ————. Fäbodväsendet i Övre Dalarna. Stockholm: Akademilittertur, 1977.
114. ————. Leksands fäbodar. Falun: privately printed, 1975.
115. ————. "Ore sockens fäbodar." In Ore—Socknen och kommunen. ed. Georg Landberg. Malung: privately printed, 1977, pp. 37-97.
116. Nylen, Anna-Maja. Swedish Handcraft. Trans. Anne-Charlotte Harvey. New York: Van Nostrand Reinhold, 1977.
117. Nyman, Anders. Hur står det till med vara fäbodar? En redogörelse för Nordiska museets fäbodinventering. n.p., n.d.
118. Reinton, Lars. Säterbruket i Norge. Oslo: n.p., 1955.
119. Rosander, Göran. En leksandssågare i Stockholm. Falun: Dalarana museum, 1972.
120. ————. Dalska arbetsvandringar före nya tidens genombrott. Stockholm: Institutet för folklivs-forskning, 1979.
121. ————, ed. Nordiskt fäbodväsen. Stockholm: Nordis-ka museet, 1977.
122. Svärdström, Svante. Dalmålningar i urval. Stockholm: Bonniers, 1975.
123. von Sydow, Carl W. "Folktale Studies and Philology: Some Points of View." In The Study of Folklore. Ed. Alan Dundes. Englewood Cliffs: Prentice-Hall, 1965, pp. 219-242.
124. Szabo, Matyas. Herdar och husdjur. Nordiska museets hanglingar, No. 73. Lund: Nordiska museet, 1970.
125. Thompson, Stith, ed. Motif Index of Folk Literature. 6 Vols. Bloomington: Indiana University Press, 1955.
126. Thyselius, Thorborg. Fäbodvall. Stockholm: Raben och Sjögren, 1963.
127. Tillhagen, Carl-Herman. Folklig läkekonst. Stockholm: Bonniers, 1962.
128. Veirulf, Olle. Orsa, en sockenbeskrivning. 2 Vols. Stockholm: privately printed, 1953.
129. Yoder, Don. "Folk Medicine." In Folklore and Folk-life. ed. Richard M. Dorson. Chicago: University of Chicago Press, 1972, pp. 191-215.